Arianna Snow's

The Lochmoor Glen Series

"Patience, My Dear by Arianna Snow is a reader engaging romantic mystery novel in which lead character, Naomi, questionably finds her first love, Hiram, after 18 years of separation. Providing the reader with seemingly endless twists and turns of plot, *Patience, My Dear* is an enthralling, well crafted, superbly written 'page-turner' of a read, fruitfully exposed to the impairing remembrance and encounter of a first young love when nearing mid-life many years later. *Patience, My Dear* is very strongly recommended for readers searching for a superbly authored telling of an intricate and entertaining tale involving a love consumed memory and an ever-deepening mystery."

"The sequel to *Patience, My Dear*, *My Magic Square*, which follows the adventures of Hiram McDonnally, debonair individual who returns to a small village in 1913 Scotland only to discover a tangled mix of dishonesty, intrigue, star-crossed love, and eroding trust among the villagers. A comedy of errors held together with taut suspense and biting dialogue, *My Magic Square* is a delicious pleasure from beginning to end. Naomi, the heroine of *Patience, My Dear*, also returns in this "must-read" sequel for all who delighted in the previous volume."

"Unwelcome visitors make their residence nearby, and there's a reason why they're unwelcome. *Threaded Needles* follows two amateur detectives whose bond of blood is unbreakable as they try to find out just what suspicious character Ian MacGill and his associate are planning. The resulting adventure is entertaining and enthralling. *Threaded Needles* is highly recommended for community library mystery collections."

"Dreams are to be treasured as they are pursued, and mourned when they are lost. *'Blessed Petals'* is a novel of dreams and how some succeed, while others are shattered. A compelling human drama unfolds, making *'Blessed Petals'* a very solidly recommended read all the way through."

—Midwest Book Review

Without a Sword

A NOVEL

Arianna Snow

Golden Horse Ltd.
Cedar Rapids, Iowa

This book is primarily a book of fiction. Names, characters, places and incidents are either products of the author's imagination or actual historic places and events which have been used fictitiously for historical reference as noted.

An *Original Publication of Golden Horse Ltd.*
P.O. Box 1002
Cedar Rapids, IA 52406-1002 U.S.A.
www.ariannaghnovels.com
ISBN 10: 0-9772308-6-4
ISBN 13: 9780977230860

Library of Congress Control Number: 2009927316
First Printing
Volume 7 of The Lochmoor Glen Series

Printed and bound in the United States of America
by Publishers' Graphics, LLC: Carol Stream, IL

Cover: Design by Arianna Snow
        Photography by EZ
        Kite designs by L.S. McClenahan
        Layout by CEZ
        Printed by White Oak Printing, Lancaster, PA

♥

In memory
of
our precious gray tabby,
the last of the four

Heidi

My Special thanks to:
God

my husband
everything

KAE, LC, CE
editorial

our babies, grandbabies, relatives and friends
support

Momma and Daddy, LC
for bookkeeping and packaging

LC
word-processing
♥

HIRAM GEOFFREY MCDONNALLY FAMILY TREE

PATERNAL GRANDPARENTS
CAPTAIN GEOFFREY EDWARD MCDONNALLY
CATHERINE NORTON MCDONNALLY

FATHER
CAPTAIN GEOFFREY LACHLAN MCDONNALLY

UNCLE
EDWARD CALEB MCDONNALLY

MATERNAL GRANDPARENTS
ALEXANDER THOMAS SELRACH
SARAH GLASGOW SELRACH

MOTHER
AMANDA SELRACH MCDONNALLY

SISTER
HANNAH RUTH MCDONNALLY

NIECE
SOPHIA MCDONNALLY

CARETAKERS
ALBERT ZIGMANN
ELOISE ZIGMANN

SON - GUILLAUME ZIGMANN

FRIEND: TRINA DUNMORE

FRIENDS
DANIEL O'LEARDON
RAHZVON SIERZIK

LIVIA NICHOLS

NAOMI BEATRICE (MACKENZIE) MCDONNALLY FAMILY TREE

PATERNAL GRANDPARENTS
JEREMIAH NORMAN MACKENZIE
OCTAVIA HILL MACKENZIE

FATHER
NATHAN ELIAS MACKENZIE
DAGMAR ARNOLDSON MACKENZIE (STEPMOTHER)

MATERNAL GRANDPARENTS
JAMES HENRY SMITHFIELD
IRENE CLEBOURNE SMITHFIELD

MOTHER
BEATRICE SMITHFIELD MACKENZIE

BROTHER
JEREMIAH JAMES MACKENZIE

DAUGHTER
ALLISON SARAH O'CONNOR

HUSBAND
EDWARD CALEB MCDONNALLY

HALF-BROTHER
HENRY STRICKLAND (SON OF CECIL AND BEATRICE)
(WIFE: PEARL   SONS: MARVIN, CONRAD)

FRIENDS
HARRIET DUGAN
JOSEPH DUGAN
HENRY MCTAVISH

MARYANNE AND BRUCE WHEATON
DAUGHTERS:
  WILMOTH, MARVEL, CORINNE, JEANIE, DARA, MARTHA

The Chapters

Chapter 1

"Shilling for Your Thoughts"

"The wondrous moment of our meeting ...
I well remember you appear
Before me like a vision fleeting,

A beauty's angel pure and clear."

— Alexander Pushkin

Naomi McDonnally sat at her dressing table at Brachney Hall, brushing her hair and pondering her last disastrous meeting with Hiram—her childhood sweetheart and now, nephew by her marriage to his uncle.

If only Hiram would have listened to me, he would have known that I located Livia—right there in London, she lamented. Ignorant of the fact that Hiram and Livia had actually met during his visit to Town, Naomi resolved to try again to inform him when he returned to Lochmoor Glen.

"Good morning, Love," Edward greeted her from the bedroom doorway.

"Good morning, my wonderful husband," Naomi replied cheerily, powdering her nose.

"The girls and I were beginning to wonder if you got lost in one of your mysteries." He noted the copy of *A Study in Scarlet* on the bureau.

I was, she thought. "I am moving a bit slower than usual today."

"Are you not well?" he asked with more than average concern.

"No, I am well."

"No uncommon queasiness this morning?"

"No...why do you ask *Edward?*" She looked at him dubiously.

Edward shrugged with innocence.

"In due time, my darling; you are frightfully impatient," Naomi sympathized.

"A minor McDonnally failing. You shan't find a patient one among us—Hiram, Sophia, myself." He walked over to the bed and stroked Patience, who purred gratefully. "Naomi, there is something that I need to tell you. Albert returned with Hannah last evening."

"Hiram's twin is here in Lochmoor Glen?" She laid down the brush. "But wait—Sophia has gone with our Allison and the others to visit with her in Paris."

"Actually, before they left for France, they coincidentally met Hannah at the port."

Naomi slipped on her shoes. "Indeed? What perfect timing. I suppose that the girls were disappointed with the trip being cancelled." She followed Edward into the hall. "I have to admit that I am delighted that Allison has returned, I was missing her before she left. Is she downstairs?"

Edward walked next to her, and then stopped. "Naomi, Allison did not come home."

"Where is she, with Sophia at Hiram's?" she asked unconcerned.

"She is not in Lochmoor Glen," he said solemnly.

"*Edward*, where is she?"

"Come into the library, I shall explain."

The Wheaton girls, for whom Naomi and Edward were temporarily parenting, played outside the window. Their laughter penetrated the room until Edward pulled down the sash.

"Please sit down, Love."

"Edward, you are frightening me. Where has she gone?"

"Allison is well. Now, please, have a seat."

Naomi let out a sigh, but sat perched on the edge of the couch. "Edward what has happened? Tell me, now!" she commanded warily.

"Rahzvon."

"Rahzvon?" Naomi got up, wrung her hands and walked in a circle around her husband. "I was afraid of this. I knew it would not be long before Allison disclosed her attraction for him." She paused. "After all, Guillaume...well, Guillaume is attractive in his way, but compared to Rahzvon—well, need one say more." She passed by Edward without noticing his widened eyes. "So she has run off with him. His good sense and the control he demonstrates in his speech and his—"

"Halt!" Astonished, Edward asked, "Allison is taken with *Rahzvon*?"

Naomi shrank back, "Well, she *is* with Rahzvon, is she not?"

"Not *alone* with him. She is with Guillaume. *Naomi,* are you saying that our girl has an interest in Rahzvon? Did she confide this in you?"

Naomi's jaw dropped. "No."

"Naomi, then why did you assume that she ran away with him?"

"I only thought that when you mentioned Rahzvon...." She backed toward the window.

"Because *you* think that Rahzvon is the better catch; you expected your daughter to feel the same," he deduced with suspicion.

"Forget I mentioned it. I was mistaken."

Edward folded his arms, "I certainly hope so, or your poor baby will suffer greatly at the hand of our niece. Sophia is a McDonnally, through and through. Coming between Sophia and Rahzvon would be lethal at the very least."

"Edward, just forget that I said anything about it. Now—tell me! Where is our daughter?"

"Allison, Guillaume, Trina, Sophia and Henry McTavish have created a band of guardian angels to accompany Rahzvon to Kosdrev."

Naomi grabbed Edward's lapels, "No, Edward! You have to stop them! They will be in danger! They know nothing about such things; they are no more than children! Albert should have stopped them!"

Edward took hold of her hands, "It was not Albert's responsibility. He and Eloise tried to reason with Guillaume, but he *is* a grown man."

She pulled away and shook her finger at Edward. "I shall never forgive Rahzvon for this!"

"Rahzvon, The Perfect? *Really*, Naomi, you need to get the facts straight. You cannot blame Rahzvon; he knew nothing about it. He had boarded the ship *alone*."

Naomi wrung her hands and threw her head back, "Uh! I do not understand any of this. How foolish can they be?"

"We are the foolish ones. It seems that our clever niece conjured up the Paris visit to her mother as a cover for their trip with Rahzvon."

"That is unconscionable!"

"*That* is Sophia, a truly *creative* McDonnally."

"Allison must be furious with Sophia for deceiving her."

"Sorry to enlighten you, my dear, but your daughter knew from the beginning that the destination was Kosdrev."

"What are we going to do, Edward?" She grasped the back of the chair.

"I am not certain that there is anything that we can do. They *are* adults and can make their own decisions *and* mistakes."

Naomi smacked her hands to her cheeks. "*Hiram*...oh," her voice wilted, "*Sophia*."

"Hmm? Hiram." Edward scratched his head. "He is returning tonight."

"Edward, he shall—"

Edward shook his head, "And to think that Eloise had just finished the repairs from his last fit of rage."

Naomi stood contemplating the possibility that she may have the key to soften the blow of Sophia's deception—knowledge of Miss Nichols whereabouts. "Perhaps, if I tell him..." Naomi said thinking aloud.

"Tell him what?" Edward asked, opening his stamp album.

Yes, about Livia, she thought. Naomi immediately dismissed sharing the information of Livia with Edward. "I am certain that Hiram's anger will be diffused in finding...in finding that his sister, Hannah, has returned."

Edward embraced Naomi, "My dear, I know that once my nephew discovers Sophia's scheme and learns of Abigail's marriage, there will be nothing that anyone can say or do to tame his temper."

Not true—there is one woman. And thanks to the agency, I have located her, Naomi thought smiling hopefully.

The next day, Naomi was standing in the parlor of McDonnally Manor, speaking with Hiram's housekeeper, Eloise, when the McDonnally carriage appeared in the drive.

"Eloise, Hiram's back!"

"Mum, I must notify his sister." Eloise said, rushing down the hall.

The carriage stopped and Naomi hurried out to greet him as he stepped from the door.

"Welcome back, Hiram."

"Thank you, Naomi. And where is my fortunate uncle?"

"He is in the garden with the children."

"Aye, the perfect father figure. Now, I would like to in—"

"Hiram it is urgent that I speak with you," Naomi insisted, not noticing the presence of his traveling companion who remained seated within the carriage.

"But I have some—"

"Hiram, this really cannot wait," Naomi reiterated, knowing that it would be beneficial to tell him of the news of Livia before he learned of their niece's situation and his ex-fiancé's marriage to the Captain.

Perturbed, Hiram gave a slight frown and walked briskly behind the carriage out of the driver's earshot. Livia remained quiet in the dim confines of the carriage, trying not to eavesdrop.

"Hiram, I tried to inform you before you left to London, but you did not give me the opportunity."

"About what are you talking, Naomi?"

"Livia Nichols," Naomi announced, waiting cautiously for his response.

"Aye?" Hiram squinted curiously at Naomi's anxious expression.

"Yes, Hiram." She took his hand. "I do not know how you shall accept this news, but prepare yourself for a shock," Naomi said with compassion.

Hiram concealed his bemusement and maintained a serious expression to humor her. "I am ready."

"I found her, Hiram."

"Found who?"

"Livia Nichols!"

Hiram, confused, looked to the carriage then to Naomi. "You say that you have found her?"

"Yes, I know it is unbelievable. Because I owe you so awfully much, I was compelled to find a way to repay you. Thus, I hired a detective."

"Naomi, first, you owe me nothing. Secondly, you really had no right to search for her without my permission. Perhaps, I have no interest in finding her." He looked casually toward the carriage, his eyes twinkling.

"No interest? But she is your—you were suffering so." Naomi looked perplexed. This was not the response, which she had expected.

Hiram stepped back, folded his arms and ran his hand across his chin. He smiled to himself remembering Livia's compliment on the beard. He stared down at Naomi. "So you think that you know where this Lydia may be found."

Naomi drew a disturbed expression, "*Livia,* not Lydia."

"Lydia, Livia, what is the difference? Very well, then, where is she?" Hiram asked with little interest.

"London," Naomi reported, beginning to wonder if she knew Hiram at all.

"So you discovered she is in Town?"

"Yes. I am only sorry you were not aware of this fact while you were there."

"I do not believe it," he shook his head.

"Hiram, I understand you not wanting to accept it—but it is true. My detective confirmed it." She took a hold of his arm. "You can go back," she said with a serious tone.

"Well, I am sorry you went to all that trouble, Naomi, but it is of little importance to me, now—a couple days earlier, perhaps." He walked toward the carriage door, "Now, I have brought a guest with me."

"A guest?"

"Aye, in the carriage."

"Oh! I apologize. I did not intend to give you cause to neglect your guest," Naomi fretted.

"Naomi, after you meet this woman, you shall understand."

"A woman? But Hiram, what about Miss Nichols?" Naomi whispered.

"Naomi, trust me."

"Hiram, you have been in London, but less than a week. I do not want to interfere, but think about this—I have *found* Livia Nichols."

Hiram gave a carefree motion with his hand, "Ah, no matter—come along, I shall introduce you to someone *really* special."

Hiram opened the carriage door, poked his head inside and whispered to Livia to go along with his charade in concealing her identity. He then took her hand and helped her outside.

He smiled at his guest, "This, my love, is Naomi McDonnally, my very young aunt and dear friend."

Naomi found the woman to be truly extraordinary, but well aware that Hiram had a knack for choosing beautiful companions as Elizabeth Clayton and Abigail were proof of that. However, Naomi had to admit that this woman was in a class of her own. Her smooth facial features were soft and purely angelic. *She looks as though she could never display anger or distress,* Naomi thought, staring at the beguiling guest, taking no notice that Hiram had failed to introduce her.

"It is my great pleasure, Mrs. McDonnally. Hiram as spoken so highly of you and your husband, Edward," Livia said sweetly.

Hiram closed the door, "Shall we find *your* husband, *my* uncle, Naomi?"

The odd threesome entered the mansion and Hiram instructed a servant, "Aubrey, take her bags up to the Rose Room."

Naomi's eyes widened. *The Rose Room? No one has ever been permitted to stay in there.*

"Come along, ladies." Hiram offered an arm to each of the women and walked proudly down the hall toward the backdoor.

"Hiram?" Naomi pleaded.

"Aye, Naomi? Ah, you said Edward was entertaining the lassies in the garden."

"Yes, but—" Naomi attempted to learn his guest's name.

Hiram turned to Livia, "You do remember when I spoke of the Wheaton children?"

"Of course, Bruce and Maryanne's daughters; the parents are hospitalized."

Hiram looked to Naomi. "Is she not wonderful? She remembers the smallest details," he said proudly.

"Yes, but—"

"There he is!" Hiram said spotting Edward counting, sitting on a concrete bench with his hands over his eyes. There was no sign of the children.

Hiram looked toward Livia, "Edward. He never really grew up. He is but a child at heart."

Livia immediately noticed the difference in the appearance of the two men. Edward was much fairer and light haired. No sooner had she made the comparison, when, a tall woman stepped out from behind the hedge. She, on the other hand, was the epitome of what Livia knew to be the typical McDonnally.

"Hannah!" Hiram pulled away from Livia and Naomi, shot down the walk, and lifted his twin sister off her feet. He kissed her blushing cheeks before lowering her to the ground. Edward removed his hands to witness the tender moment while Livia and Naomi enjoyed the reunion, as well.

"You have made your brother a very happy man. Life has been exceptional of late."

"*Hiram,*" Hannah hugged him, holding back her tears. "I beg your forgiveness for Sophia's absence."

"Aye, so it is true. She has left for Kosdrev, as I suspected."

He knows about Sophia? Naomi realized.

"I tried desperately to convince her to come back with me, but that girl is as stubborn as a..." Hannah complained.

"As a McDonnally," Hiram cut in. "You shan't fret, I will be sending someone to retrieve her."

"Dear brother, that shall be difficult. She is taken with that young man, Rondon."

"*Rahzvon.* I know. If it is any consolation, he is a good man, Hannah," Hiram reassured her.

"Unfortunately, uncommonly handsome, as well."

Hiram closed his eyes briefly, "Sophia's weakness," he said, in despairing agreement. "Hannah, come. I want you to meet someone."

Hiram led Hannah over to where Edward was introducing himself to Livia. Naomi waited anxiously for the guest to disclose her identity.

"Excellent—the two of you have met," Hiram remarked.

"Not exactly. She knows my name—" Edward began.

Hannah approached Livia, "Hello, you must be Miss O'Leardon. It is Abigail?"

"No, no!" Naomi blurted, "Abigail is married to—" Edward quickly clamped his hand across Naomi's mouth and smiled at Hiram.

Hiram returned a broad smile, "There is no need for alarm, everyone. Nay, Hannah, this is not

Abigail. In fact, we met with her and her husband, Captain Latimer, in Town."

Edward raised his brows with surprise at his nephew's indifferent attitude. Naomi breathed again with relief as her husband removed his silencing hand.

Hiram placed his arm around Livia's shoulders, "Hannah, Edward," he turned and faced Naomi, "Naomi, I would like to present to you a woman very dear to my heart—Miss Livia Nichols."

Naomi's eyes nearly left her head. She looked to Livia and then to Hiram and shook her head. "You rascal!"

Hiram and Livia grinned mischievously at one another for their successful scheming.

Edward kissed Livia's hand, "Welcome to Lochmoor Glen, Miss Nichols. Why on earth would such a delightful woman accompany my ragtag, bearded nephew to this lowly estate?"

Livia laughed, admiring the grandiose façade of the mansion, "Because your handsome, tenacious nephew stood in the year's worst thunderstorm until he was drenched, carried on a lengthy conversation with an inanimate frog, and took the liberty of packing my clothing himself in order to assure my journey to his home."

Hiram stood silent as his relatives studied him. "And I would do it all again. Let us go in for tea," Hiram suggested with a proud smile.

"You will have to excuse me, for a few minutes." Edward glanced around the garden. "I have a few things to find first." He darted behind the bushes in search of the weary hide-and-seek players.

Hiram pointed out the kitchen, dining room, and the infamous grandfather clock. After a brief tour of his study, they retired to the parlor.

Once seated, Naomi turned to Livia and inquired, "How long will you be visiting in Lochmoor?"

Livia smiled shyly, "Indefinitely. I am to be the new schoolteacher."

Edward stood in the archway as his mouth dropped open. He looked toward his nervous nephew, now pacing. "*Hiram,* what has happened to Miss Nettlepin?"

"Uh...she is in Town."

Naomi looked to the face of one she knew the village children would adore, "Congratulations, Miss Nichols. It was common knowledge that Miss Nettlepin was efficient, but not favored by her pupils."

"Thank you for your vote of confidence. I know that I will thoroughly enjoy teaching in your lovely village. I cannot wait to see the school."

Now with the school burned to the ground, Edward and Naomi simultaneously looked to Hiram in question of his negligence in revealing this pertinent information to the newly appointed teacher.

"Edward, Naomi, might you join me in the kitchen to prepare tea?" Hiram looked desperately for their compliance.

"You have been gone less than a week and you have forgotten that you have servants in your employ?" Edward teased.

"*Edward,* they are new to the premises, we have to show them where we keep the tea," Hiram spoke, shooting a warning glance to his uncle.

"Incompetent help." Edward nodded and followed Hiram. Naomi did not.

"*Naomi*," Hiram insisted.

"Hiram, I think that I will stay and become better acquainted with Hannah and Livia."

Hiram forced a smile and left with Edward.

Edward put his hand on Hiram's shoulder as they walked to the kitchen. "You did very well for yourself, ol' man—in record time, no less."

"Things are not always as they appear, Edward."

"Is she not staying in Lochmoor Glen and is she not going to be our new school teacher?"

"Nay."

Edward grabbed Hiram's arm, "Hiram, you have not deceived that lovely creature? Where is Miss Nettlepin? What have you done with her?"

"Nothing, but I should have." Hiram sat down at the kitchen table and shoved the bowl of fruit to the other end. "That woman will not give me any peace."

"Miss Nichols?"

"Nettlepain," Hiram grumbled.

"Clever twist on the name, Hiram."

Hiram leaned toward Edward, "She followed me to London and presented me with an ultimatum."

"This, I do not doubt."

"She forced me to visit with her. I left her room with her unsavory promise to be waiting for me, here in Lochmoor."

"You must have made quite an impression."

Hiram threw him a contemptuous look.

"Sorry. Calm down." Edward took the chair across from Hiram when Eloise entered the kitchen.

"Sir, might I prepare tea for your guests?" she asked her master.

Hiram folded his arms on the table and dropped his head, "Nay, leave us alone."

Edward scowled, "*Hiram.* Eloise, ignore him. Please serve the guests. We will continue this discussion in the study. Come along, Hiram."

Hiram looked up and followed Edward in a self-loathing manner to the study while the three women watched through the archway as the pocket doors closed behind the mysterious men. Hannah turned to Naomi.

"They are probably discussing the situation regarding my unruly daughter." She then turned with a skeptical eye to Livia.

"Tell me Miss Nichols, what actually inspired you to return to my brother's home after knowing him only a week?" *His good looks, his money, or both?* she thought cynically.

Naomi sat in dread of the oncoming controversy, instigated by the protective sister.

"I would suppose the same inspiration that brought *you* to your brother's house—the love for a decent, caring man," Livia said casually.

Hannah sat back, and then offered a genuine smile. "That was an impressive answer, if you are truly sincere."

"I am."

"Then I approve, Miss Nichols."

"As do I."

Naomi was relieved to see the exchange of words to end pleasantly and abruptly.

In the study, Hiram was pacing and Edward was busy pondering the disagreeable situation.

"Hiram, in order to get to the root of this problem, I need to know why you offered Miss Nichols, Miss Nettlepin's job."

"Because I thought she wanted to have my children," he mumbled.

"Hiram McDonnally! You gave Livia the teaching position, in exchange for mothering your bairn? Are you *that* desperate, man?"

"Nay! We were conversing. I cannot remember how it began. She was elated about becoming the new teacher...I was confused. She was not at all clear as to what she was referring." Hiram stopped pacing and pointed his finger at Edward. "Not *once*, not once did she use the term *teacher*."

"Keep your voice down. Explain slowly. Why exactly does Livia believe that Miss Nettlepin has relinquished her position?"

"All I said was that Miss Nettlepin was out of my life."

"But *not* out of Lochmoor Glen? *Hiram*, that implication is no better than an outright lie."

"I know. I did not have the heart to tell her that there was not an available position. If you would have seen her face—it glowed like a hundred candles."

"Well, Hiram, that may be the case, but when Miss Nettlepin arrives, those cherished flames are going to be extinguished in a heartbeat."

Chapter 11

"The Dragon"

"Rich gifts wax poor
when givers prove unkind."

—William Shakespeare

"Confound it! Sack Miss Nettlepin, Edward!" Hiram demanded.

"I have no authority to do that, Hiram."

"Why not? Without the McDonnallys, there would not have been a school."

"*Hiram*, I am surprised at you. You *are* desperate. Miss Nettlepin may be a pain, but she is a good teacher and she deserves the right to remain here. My dear nephew, how do you manage to get into these sticky-wickets?"

"Am I not talking to the master of serpentine situations?"

"Aye… I have been involved in a few—so listen to me. We can remedy this situation. If you value this relationship with Miss Nichols, as much as I think you do, we can speak to Miss Nettlepin about taking on an assistant."

"My obsessive admirer shall hardly approve of having my wife for her assistant," Hiram dropped hopelessly into a chair.

"Your *wife*? Hiram, Miss Nichols is ethereal at the least, but you cannot possibly be serious! You barely know the woman. We cannot afford to cause a scandal, over one woman's desires."

Hiram pounded his fist on the desk with each word, "Livy wants to be the teacher, so she shall be!"

"Get a hold man."

"Livy is not just a woman, Edward."

"Apparently not; she seems to have cast some sort of spell upon you."

"She is perfect—Livy could never do anything wrong or deceitful. She is infallible." He walked toward the doors. "Enough said. We need to join the ladies, before Livy feels uncomfortable." He slid open the doors.

"*Hiram*," Edward pleaded.

Hiram smiled at the three women who turned to watch them exiting the study. Eloise flashed an approving smile toward Hiram for his choice of the new guest and left the women in the parlor with a tray of sweets and tea.

"Miss Nichols, where was your last teaching position?" Hannah asked.

"Actually, I have never been given the opportunity, until now." She smiled gratefully at Hiram. He half-smiled and glanced at Edward who tightened his lips and looked away, bewildered.

"What is your chosen subject, Livia?" Naomi asked eagerly.

"I have a preference for writing and literature."

"But of course! I understand that you wrote a novel," Naomi said with interest.

Naomi's response jogged Hiram's memory. Livia had mentioned authoring a novel in one of her many notes. He wondered how Naomi knew this. He suddenly remembered, *her hired detective.*

"Not really a novel... a novelette. May I inquire as to how you discovered this?" Livia asked.

"Why Sophia, Hiram's niece—Hannah's daughter has a copy."

Hannah, Edward and Hiram all exchanged looks of surprise. Livia looked fearfully to the floor.

Naomi continued to explain to her very curious audience. "The book was actually a gift from Rahzvon."

Hannah gave a distressed headshake with mention of Rahzvon's connection with Sophia.

Naomi stood proudly before the group. "Before Sophia left to Par— before she left, she came to me with the novel—*novelette.*"

"Does Sophia speak Italian?" Livia asked anxiously.

"Not a word, but she knows her French," Hannah chimed in.

Livia gave a sigh of relief, which confused Hiram.

You Livy? What could you have included in this novel that is not fit for my niece? Hiram thought.

Naomi turned to Livia, "Sophia's inability to translate the text was not a problem. Rahzvon is fluent in Italian."

Hannah shifted uneasily with mention of Sophia's suitor, once again. Livia stared down at her hands and clutched her purse.

Hiram observed the mysterious author. *Of what is she afraid?* His gaze was broken when Naomi addressed him.

"Sir, how does it feel to be the honorary character in a novel? Not everyone has that rare opportunity to see their name in print," Naomi asked, sharing in the pride of being a member of his clan. Hiram's eyes narrowed, as did Edward's in fearful anticipation of his wife's upcoming report.

Naomi explained further, "Sophia would have never shared this discovery with me, if Livia had chosen another name for her character. At first, I thought it impossible, but when Sophia revealed Rahzvon's translation of the character's description—yours, Hiram—Sophia and I knew that odds were against two *Hirams* sharing an identical physical description. I am a great lover of myster..." Naomi paused, seeing the disturbed faces—Livia's fearful expression and Hiram's brewing rage. Naomi looked to Edward for assistance.

He obliged by leaning over and whispering to her, "Love, you are now an official triple "M".

Naomi squinted with confusion.

"Misspoken McDonnally Misfit."

"What?"

"It just came off the top of my head." Edward shrugged.

Naomi turned to see Hiram leaving his chair and walking to the window where he snatched hold of the drapes and asked through clenched teeth, "Excuse me, Naomi...could you please provide me with the title of this novel, again? I seem to have forgotten."

Naomi hesitated in observing Livia's closed eyelids. Edward gave Naomi a warning nod to continue. She swallowed. "I believe it was...*If Only We had Kissed.*"

There was a deafening silence. All eyes traced Hiram's path to the new Windsor chair—all, except Livia's. He grasped the back of the chair, sending shivers down the spines of his observers, who held their breath preparing for its demolition. Instead, Hiram turned to Livia.

"Am I to understand that you wrote a novel about me, entitled *If Only We had Kissed*?" he asked pointedly.

Livia, unprepared for Hiram's blatant disapproval, left her chair in flight.

"Livia, do not dare—no crying!" Hiram shouted shaking his finger at her.

The others in the room, watched uncomfortably. Hiram's warning had no merit; Livia broke down. He reached up, clutched his curls with frustration and let out a low frustrated growl.

"Livy, aye, I am angry, very angry, but I am *not* leaving you. I am going to...to check on the horses," he said abruptly. He turned to Naomi who held Livia trembling in her arms.

He turned on his way out, "Do not allow her to leave this room under any circumstances. Excuse me." He disappeared abruptly through the archway.

No one knew what to say. A faint distant bellow from the direction of the barn preceded Edward's announcement, "Welcome home, Hannah. There goes the barn."

Naomi empathized with Livia and felt certain remorse for mentioning the novel. In her dread of Hiram's return, Livia struggled to review every line of defense for creating the book. Hannah sat unshaken, realizing that her brother had not changed since that day he destroyed the door of the café, when she refused to return home with him. Edward excused himself and left to check on the condition of the barn and his irate nephew.

He approached the barn, silent of any turmoil. He peeked in to see Hiram standing amidst the floor strewn with demolished bales and assorted tack.

"Has the storm passed?" Edward asked.

"How is she?"

"The *infallible* woman?"

Hiram glared at Edward who quickly reported, "She stopped crying."

Edward entered and began gathering up the bridles. "Who is she Hiram?"

"I knew her in Switzerland, ten years ago." He put his hands on his hips, staring obliviously at the mess he created. "Edward, I cannot believe that there is a book floating around out there, revealing all of my weaknesses. Worse yet, it was authored by the woman I love more than life itself." He looked up at Edward, "Can you believe that she told the entire world that I never had the nerve to kiss her?"

"Not *a* book—*Books*. There may be dozens, possibly thousands."

For Edward's sake, it was definitely beneficial that looks cannot kill.

Edward then defensively offered some immediate consolation, "Hiram, it *is* written in Italian."

Hiram ignored his attempt. "You know as well as I, that when it comes to the society columns, nothing is sacred—the McDonnally clan or any other. Someone will discover it and everyone will be laughing from here to Hong Kong. Imagine the headlines." He shook his head and kicked an overturned bale.

"*Every Lady's Man Afraid of Every Lady?*" Edward offered.

Hiram sneered at him.

"Ol' chap, you are taking this entirely too seriously. What does it matter if word gets out? Have her write a sequel, a rebuttal, if you will. However, if you do not return to the house shortly and apologize, you may find yourself to be the inspiration for yet another book, *If only He had Mercy.* Come along lad, your *perfect* lady awaits. You had better make amends, the competition has returned."

"Who?"

"Zedidiah Hartstrum—the topic of choice of every woman in Scotland." Edward hung up the last bridle.

"I *never* believed that was his *real* name." Hiram walked to the window. "What are they saying?"

"The usual— 'not a kinder, gentler, sweeter, man tread the earth.' Even Naomi gave an interested sigh when Eloise mentioned his arrival." Edward led the way from the barn to the garden. "The unmarried women, and some of the unscrupulous married ones, will be storming the mercantile in search of the latest fragrances and fashions to impress the man. It happens every time he lands in Lochmoor Glen. Last year, Elsa Huggins abandoned her husband and children to follow him to Zimbabwe. Of course, being the decent chap that he is, he sent her back. Zed may not have our physical appeal, Hiram, but the man can out charm the lot of us."

"What brings the arrogant beggar to Lochmoor?" Hiram said, grasping the gate.

"He was summoned to organize the financial affairs for rebuilding the *school*. By the way, how does Miss Nichols feel about your temper tantrums?"

Hiram said nothing and slammed the gate closed behind them.

"I thought so. She is too mild-mannered to approve." Edward gave a hopeless sigh. "Zed has never raised *his* voice."

"I am not at all concerned with the likes of that sanctimonious simpleton. He must be an old man by now," Hiram grumbled while they continued down the garden path.

"Not unless you think that I am an *old* man. He was in my class; remember? He stole Emma Stafford away from me in less time than it took to drink a cup of tea. You *are* aware that some women prefer older men."

Hiram snarled at the thought when Naomi flew from the back door and announced, "Excuse me, but I think that it is imperative that you hurry inside, Hiram. Miss Nichols is determined to leave."

"I asked you to keep her there." Hiram complained shooting past Naomi and through the door. He moved swiftly down the hall to the parlor where Hannah and Eloise were doing their best to detain Livia.

"Thank you ladies, but I need to speak with Miss Nichols."

Eloise led Hannah from the room. "Come along, Mum. I want to show you the cottage. Master, dinner shall be served at seven."

"Thank you, Eloise."

"Livy, please sit down. I promise to remain calm and rational."

Livia sat.

"Why in the name of—why did you do it?" Hiram chastised.

"Hiram do not shout at me—I am leaving."

"Livy," he explained returning her to her seat, "I was not shouting—I was speaking with emphasis. I apologize." He took a breath and folded his hands. "Please, tell me why you would humiliate me, making me the laughing stock of the entire world." He took another breath. "I shall give it my best go to understand."

"Hiram, I wrote that book *three years* ago," she defended.

"Three *years*?" he asked with renewed interest.

"Hiram, I told you that I have never stopped thinking about you. In fact, that is why I wrote the book. A friend of mine, who was studying human behavior, convinced me that it would help me accept my loss of our relationship, if I were to write about you."

"Granted, it may have been therapeutic, but why did you need to publish it?"

Livy did not reply.

"Livy, I want an answer."

"You want an answer? Very well...I thought that, by chance, if God wanted us to find each other again, my novel may lead you to me."

"And you knew that I studied Italian, insuring that I could read it."

"Yes. It is not written in English. I thought that would protect you from the British masses."

"But Livia, how did you ever expect me to stumble upon this book?"

"Divine providence. And you see, you did."

"*Livy*, I found you without the aid of the book."

"That was purely coincidental."

Livia's reasoning was more complex and convoluted than Hiram cared to analyze. He took a deep breath, offering Livia his arm.

"Let me show you to your room." As they ascended the stairs, Hiram asked, "Livy, do you have a copy of the novel with you?"

"*Novelette*. I do."

"I would like one, please."

"For what purpose?" she asked skeptically.

"A man cannot fight a dragon without a sword."

"It really is harmless, Hiram."

"That, Miss Nichols, shall be for me to judge."

"As Naomi inferred, perhaps you will be immortalized," Livia offered weakly.

"Aye, like Michelangelo's *David,* with my private life stark-naked to the world."

Livia rolled her eyes and followed Hiram into the Rose Room.

Chapter 111

"*Redemption*"

"'Tis strange,—but true;
for Truth is always strange—
stranger than fiction: if it could be told,
How much would novels
gain by the exchange!
How differently the World
would men behold!"

—Lord Byron

"Hiram, it is glorious, breathtaking. It is so elegant," Livia gazed around the brightly lit room.

"Other than Hannah and Sophia, and the cleaning staff, of course, no other person has seen this room, since my mother's passing. Everything in it belonged to her. Many are inherited and several are gifts from my father. This was not her bedchamber; it is located on the third floor. This was originally her private sitting room."

Livia admired the enchanting retreat. She moved to the dressing table and carefully chose the crystal perfume atomizer. After a sniff, she replaced it next to the pincushion donning a dozen or more hatpins, which were adorned with various gemstones and beads.

"May I?" she asked. Hiram nodded. She opened the satin-lined glove box that held assorted hair combs and shell hairpins, rather than gloves. "Lovely." She closed the lid and approached the bookshelf on the far wall. She ran her finger down the spine of the leather bound novel, *Emma,* when her gaze fell to the copy of *Graham's Magazine* on the night table. She picked it up and thumbed through it. Hiram's thoughts returned to her novel.

"Poe's, *The Murders in the Rue Morgue*," she read.

"Ah, assassination; how timely. Only we were discussing *character* assassination." He raised a brow.

"*Hiram.*" She gave a subtle headshake of annoyance.

"Now, do whatever it is that you women do to prepare yourself for dinner. I need to make some arrangements to have Sophia brought safely back to Lochmoor and to her senses."

"I truly am greatly honored to be a guest in this room." Livia went to her bag, pulled a copy of her book from it, and handed it to Hiram. He looked at it skeptically while Livia prayed that he would not find its contents to be unacceptable.

"Thank you, Livy. I shall see you in the dining room." Hiram closed the door and went downstairs where he met Edward in the hall.

"All is well?" Edward asked.

"Aye, she is preparing for dinner. Come speak with me in the study. I need to confer with you in regard to Sophia."

Hiram placed the questionable account on the desk while Edward closed the doors and began, "Hiram, as I told Naomi, I am not certain that we can—is that the book?" He picked up the small dark-red leather bound novel.

"Aye. She would have to choose *red* to draw attention to it," Hiram said disdainfully.

"It is quite appealing. I wish that I shared your ability to read Italian." Edward thumbed through the pages.

"She may be sorry that *I* can read it."

"Be open-minded, Hiram. You may find it to be very complimentary." Edward placed it back on the table.

Hiram glanced away and scowled dubiously.

Edward took a seat by the fireplace. "As I was saying, I do not think that we can force our young adventurers to return. They are all adults."

"Sophia is younger than the others. She is not yet twenty and I shall not let her risk her life for anyone."

"What are you proposing?" Edward crossed his legs.

"I will hire the couple that Joseph Dugan employed to retrieve his niece from Spain."

"You are aware that Sophia shall despise us for our intervention?"

"So be it. At least she shall live to display her anger." Hiram sat down across from him.

"What do you know about Kosdrev?"

"Mountainous, rocky, and crawling with despicable despots. Time is short. We need to find them before they cross the border."

"Did you inform Hannah?" Edward asked.

"I did not want to alarm her. I only mentioned that we would have Sophia returned."

Edward thought for a minute. "I can request that Joseph get the contact information of the couple. Besides, I have to speak with him about a carpentry project."

"Project?"

"I am commissioning Joseph to construct a dollhouse for the lassies."

"You will be a model father someday, Edward... as you have been for Allison."

"Some model. Allison is out there in danger, with no thanks to me."

"Allison has a mind of her own and there is no question that you are excellent with the Wheaton children."

"I admit that 'tis not an easy task. There are *five* of them." Edward stood up. "Now, Naomi and I should be going to check on our brood."

"Ah, 'tis nothing. Livy and I are going to have six." Hiram left his chair to follow.

Edward raised his brows in wonder.

The evening meal was served as scheduled with only Hiram, his sister and Livia in attendance.

The conversation was limited to discussion of Hannah's journey from Paris. The three retired early in respect for Livia's long day of travel. Hiram did not object, having the prospect of a few hours alone with Livia's novelette.

After bidding the two women 'goodnight', Hiram sought peace in his study. After trying out two chairs, Hiram settled down in the wingback next to the fireplace and opened *If Only We Had Kissed*.

He read the dedication page, which translated to:

> *To our unspoken love—you, me, "the sand and sea."*

Her words briefly touched his heart. He read on.

> *One drifts through time, never knowing from day to day when that person will appear who will forever alter one's life.*
>
> *This is an account of such an occurrence. Albeit brief, so was the period of time, which I spent with this extraordinary individual.*

"Extraordinary? Naturally—the only man on earth who was fool enough to not kiss her," he frowned and read on.

> *In traveling with my father, I had ample time in which to explore the shops of the cities throughout this vast world. One autumn day, my father asked me to deliver our mantle clock to a local repair shop. The name of said shop and the city of its location is of no consequence.*
>
> *I entered the shop where I met a handsome, tall, young man at the counter. He was one of those few men that would catch the*

eye of every woman, young and old alike. I shall never forget his wild black curls and his daunting, large frame. However, the eyes offered the greatest impression.

Hiram smoothed his beard, noting how strange it was to read Livia's personal thoughts and to imagine the thousands of strangers that may have read them, as well. He wondered as to why so many were taken with his appearance, as he truly believed—that which is inside, is all that is important. He continued reading.

His dark eyes drew me into his troubled soul and his entrapped spirit. And yet, within minutes, I felt as though this person had brought new significance and a new beginning to my relatively empty life.

Hiram's interest grew with each additional sentence. He continued reading slowly, as his Italian suffered from lack of practice in translation.

Suddenly, he sat up from his sprawling position. The words that he dreaded appeared before him.

Hiram and I spent nearly a fortnight of afternoons together and yet, not once, did he attempt to kiss me. He often spoke positively of my appearance, so I did not have reason to believe that he did not find me to be attractive.

No more an honorable gentleman ever lived. I do believe that he respected me and, yes, truly loved me as much as I loved him. I found his traditional values refreshing, at first, but often wondered if we would be together today, if only we had kissed.

Hiram scowled at his suggested failure and tightened his grip on the book.

Although he was very open in his confessions of his past, his hopes and fears, I honestly believe that he was shy and withdrawn from displays of affection. His inexperience with women prevented him from offering so much as an embrace.

"Not true!" Hiram blurted, remembering the time he hugged her when she spoke of the missing pollywog. In his growing anger, he finished the book, which offered accounts of their moments together and her philosophical thoughts.

The following account reveals the daily activities of innocent love and friendship in a world, foreign to both Hiram and I.

At last, he reached Livia's final confession.

I felt shamefully improper for desiring my first kiss from the man, being only seventeen.
Needless to say, our farewell was also void of any such passion, although I shared a thousand kisses with this man in my hours of dreaming slumber in the years to follow our departure. I resigned to avoid any indulgence of the kind with any man who I did not love as deeply as my dear friend and loving companion who I met in the clock shop, nearly seven years past.

Hiram sat brooding.

"Shy! So, the world thinks I am shy and inexperienced. I shall show them!" Hiram tossed the book on the table and plowing through the doors, he entered the hall. His pounding boots on the steps echoed to the opposite wing. He moved directly to Livia's door and rapped violently.

"Livia, open this door! Livy, I said open this door or I am coming in!"

Livy moved quickly to the door.

"Hiram what has happened?" she asked urgently.

"I want to—to speak with you, Livia."

"But I am in my night clothing."

"Make haste. Put on something."

Livia flew to the wardrobe, slipped on her robe and slippers and fled for the door. She cracked it open. He pushed it open further and stepped inside, staring down at her.

"You think me shy?" he asked furiously.

"No—not anymore." She backed away.

"Come back here," he demanded.

Livia stood frozen and confused by what she deemed to be an extremely irrational response to her book. She began to tremble. Hiram observed the small figure when Sophia's words crept from his memory. *Rahzvon said that a gentleman would never kiss a lady in her night clothing.*

Hiram stirred uneasily then slowly turned with his back to her, "Get dressed—in something, something more appropriate." His urge to step into the hall to give her some privacy, gave way to his ego. He did not want to appear as though he had made another error in judgment, so he stood firm. Livia returned to the wardrobe to gather the necessary articles and dressed quickly behind the screen.

"Please, do not dawdle, Livy."

"Hiram, I do not understand you. You invite me into your home and the very first day, you nearly knock down my door and frighten me to death."

"Livy, I am not interested in your comments on my behavior. I have read enough of them to last me a lifetime."

"I am dressed, Hiram."

Hiram turned around ready to prove himself— to defend his honor as a man. "*Shy,* is it?" He stepped in front of her boldly.

"Hiram, yes, you *were* shy back then."

"And now? What do you think?" he demanded.

"I think that you have matured."

"Are you certain of that?"

"*Hiram.*"

He reached down and grasped her waist when he noticed that her third button of her blouse was not fastened. He removed his hands immediately and turned around.

Shocked by his quick move, Livia asked, "Hiram, what is wrong?"

"Your blouse," he mumbled.

"What did you say?"

"Your blouse."

"You do not like it?"

"The button," he whispered.

"The button?" She looked down to see it open revealing absolutely *nothing.* She smiled. *Not shy? You sweet boy,* she thought. She buttoned it. "Sir, I am decent, now."

Hiram turned back with the wind out of his sails, and at a complete loss of what to say.

"Hiram, you wanted to speak with me?"

In seeing her clothing strewn on the bed, he quickly suggested, "Aye, please come out into the hall, where we can have some privacy."

Livia squinted curiously and followed.

"Livia, I finished your novel," he said tersely.

"*Novelette*. Did you enjoy it?"

"It kept my interest," he said pointedly, folding his arms across his chest.

"Is that your reason for this unexpected visit?" Livy smiled sweetly up at him.

"Aye." Weakening, he lowered his arms.

She took his hand. "Hiram, I do not mind at all. To think that you were compelled to come to me immediately to express your gratitude, instead of waiting until morning."

Hiram looked down at her hand fastened to his. He thought that she had successfully derailed his plan to redeem himself, until she asked, "Would you like to kiss me, Hiram?"

Hiram fell hopelessly under her spell and kissed her. Livia opened her eyes and smiled, pleased with his gift of thanks. "You are welcome." She slipped from his embrace. "I shall see you at breakfast. Good night, Hiram." She turned before closing the door. "Oh, Hiram, might I ask you a question?"

"Aye?"

"What do you know of this man, Zedidiah Hartstrum?"

Chapter IV

"Stampede"

"Then talk not of inconstancy.
False hearts, and broken vows;
If I, by miracle can be
This livelong moment true to thee,
'Tis all that heaven allows."

—John Wilmot

Zedidiah Hartstrum arrived in Lochmoor Glen, shortly after one o'clock that following afternoon. An hour later, every female north of the Scotland border was aware of this rare event. Single women, sixteen to sixty, were busy with preparations to meet this distinguished visitor. While mothers were assisting their daughters in the ritual to present their finest appearance, older prospects were experimenting with new hairstyles and baking sweet offerings. All the unmarried contestants were engaged in this challenge to win Mr. Hartstrum's affections, with exception of the schoolteacher, Miss Nettlepin. As promised, she returned to Lochmoor Glen with eyes for only one man,—Hiram McDonnally—who she knew to be free of his commitment to Abigail O'Leardon.

Beatrice, Naomi's mother, found it all very amusing. "People certainly make a fuss over this man," she addressed Naomi, who was rocking the Wheaton infant.

"They do, Mother, but you need to understand that single men of good manners and moderate fortune are scarce in this part of the country," Naomi explained. "There are thrice as many women as men. His reputation is a tempting lure. I would not be surprised if Daniel were to return to protect his investment."

"*Naomi,* even this Mr. Hartstrum could not hold a candle to my sweet Daniel."

"I know that, but I am not sure that Daniel believes it. Even Edward is unnerved with the man's presence in Lochmoor, and we are happily married." Naomi placed the sleeping baby in the cradle. "Mother, what is your opinion of Livia?"

"From what you tell me, she is extremely sensitive." Beatrice gently rocked the cradle.

"Yes, she appears to be made of porcelain. I think she will break very easily. It is strange seeing Hiram with her, instead of Abigail. She was so feisty and high-spirited. Livia seems to be quite the opposite."

"From what I know of Hiram, I think that Miss Nichols may be a blessing. He needs someone sweet and genteel to draw forth that side of him," Beatrice observed.

"Possibly; Livia reminds me of one of those quaint shops in Town shelved with yards of delicate lace, French soaps and aromatic dried flowers. After having been with Abigail, who was more in tune with the Running of the Bulls in Spain, I cannot imagine Hiram content to be trapped in a tranquil shop with the scent of lavender."

Beatrice laughed at her daughter's analogy. "I still believe that she may be the solution to Hiram's idiosyncrasies."

"Mother, I do not want to be critical of the woman, but she seems to lack any depth. I am not certain that she bears the strength to tolerate Hiram's erratic behavior."

"Mark my words, my instincts tell me that Miss Nichols governs with a kind tenderness, instead of an iron fist."

"Time will tell." Naomi covered the baby with the blanket. "Livia is very much like Zed. Once Zed discovers this, I am not certain how controllable Hiram shall be. This is one village meeting that our residents may remember for a very long time." She tucked the blanket around little Dara. "You are coming?"

"My dear daughter, do you really think that I would forego this opportunity to meet this superior male who, I have been told, is a cross between Adonis and St. Nicholas?"

"*Adonis?*" Naomi laughed. Was he not killed by Aphrodite's husband, disguised as a boar?" She stood up and stretched. "Yes, I suppose the entire village shall be in attendance for one reason or another."

Dressed in one of his finest suits, Hiram paced in his bedroom. With his beard freshly trimmed, he was physically ready for the meeting. However, his confidence was definitely wavering. Not only was he leery of the presence of the guest of honor and Zedidiah's possible impression on Livia, but he was equally dreading contact with the obsessive Miss Nettlepin. In order to remain in Livia's good graces, he resigned to the fact that he had to confess to her that there, in fact, was no available teaching position in Lochmoor Glen. He stopped pacing and sat down on the bed. He could not risk, Livia learning the truth at the meeting and losing her to the predatory, Mr. Hartstrum.

"I have to do it. I have to tell her, right now." He slapped his thighs and left to end the deception. He stood outside of Livia's bedchamber gathering his courage when he heard her speaking within. He leaned closer to hear Livia's seemingly distressed voice.

"I have warned you for the last time. Do not move—not one inch closer!"

An angry, fearful expression fled across Hiram's face. His heart pounded in his ears, nearly preventing his ability to decipher her next words.

"Please stop, I beg you! I do not want to end your life!"

At that moment, raging, Hiram kicked in the

door. It flew, unhinged to the floor. There he saw Livia, alone, armed with only a single shoe.

"*Hiram,* what have you done? Why did you not knock? The door was unlocked."

Hiram rushed to the other side of the bed in search of the intruder. He got down and inspected under the bed when Livia let out a scream.

"Look out! He is running this way!" Hiram jumped to his feet and Livia jumped up on the bed, still clutching her shoe. Hiram swung around in confusion.

"Where?" he shouted.

"There!" she pointed to an inch-long, black spider racing across the tapestry rug.

Hiram looked with brief curiosity at the terrified woman, and then ended the invader's loathsome life with one slow direct move of his boot.

"There, he is dead," Hiram proudly announced.

"Hiram, you killed him!" Livia said covering her mouth.

Hiram looked up to see the startled faces of Hannah and Eloise in the doorway, reeling from the announced murder. They fearfully imagined the victim's limp body on the opposite side of the bed. Hiram sensed their fear and sought immediately to remedy it.

"It is safe, now. I smashed the culprit with my mighty boot."

Livia looked regretfully at him, "But Hiram, I did not expect you to kill him."

This was all that Eloise could endure. In her mind, her Master's temper had reached its limit. She gasped and fainted to the floor.

Hiram and Livia abandoned the eight-legged victim and hurried to assist Hannah with Eloise.

Now, the stoic, twin sister was becoming increasingly pale. "Hiram, how could you?"

Hiram quickly defended his chivalric duty, "It was only a spider, Hannah."

"*Only* a spider?" Livia mumbled as they carried Eloise to the bed. "He did not deserve to die."

Hannah breathed a sigh of relief and fanned the awaking housekeeper.

Down the road, Naomi was searching for a missing earring to wear to the six-thirty meeting. The maid knocked on her bedroom door and presented two letters, which the postman had delivered. Naomi leisurely opened the one addressed to her, noting that the London address was that of the detective agency. She began reading.

> *Mrs. McDonnally,*
>
> *I hope this letter finds you well. I am writing in regard to the first letter that I sent to you. I need to amend my findings. Miss Livia Nichols is no longer residing in London.*

Naomi rolled her eyes and continued.

> *Prepare yourself—she is apparently visiting in your village—in your nephew's home.*

Naomi shook her head. "To think I actually have to pay you for this information." She scanned down to the bottom of the page. *What do I owe you?*

The sum was fair enough. Then her curiosity got the best of her. She gingerly opened the second envelope addressed to her husband, noting it, too, was from the detective agency. She began reading.

Mr. McDonnally, if you could pay the additional balance for my services rendered for locating Beatrice MacKenzie, it would be greatly appreciated.

Mother? Naomi reread the note and sat down. She came to the realization that her mother's presence at her wedding was apparently not a mere coincidence in Daniel's bringing Beatrice to Lochmoor Glen. Edward had obviously hired an investigator to surprise Naomi with her missing mother of twelve years. *I cannot believe it—I never so much as thanked him.*

"Edward! Edward!" she ran downstairs, through the hall to the kitchen where she heard him speaking. She found him bandaging young Corinne's finger.

"What has happened?" she asked with concern.

Edward pointed his finger at the patient, "Someone was trying to cut an apple by herself."

"Me, mum," Corinne admitted, holding up her wrapped finger.

Naomi looked down at her, "Corinne, I gave you girls specific instructions to ask if you needed anything cut. The cook keeps those knives sharpened."

"Should I ask someone to cut me finger, next time," Corinne giggled.

"Silly goose," Naomi lifted the little girl's finger and kissed it. "I want you to give it a good soaking in the bath tonight. Now, go out and play."

Corrine ran outside to join her sisters.

"Edward," Naomi took his hand, "come with me to the library. I want to speak with you." She could barely wait to thank him for finding her mother.

Edward dropped the roll of gauze and grinned, believing that the moment for which he had been praying, had arrived. Naomi had a secret which she was about to reveal. *I am going to be a father,* he thought, following her down the hall. Naomi closed the door and turned smiling at her husband.

"Edward, there are not words to express my gratitude. I have waited for twelve long years."

"Gratitude?" Edward smiled proudly, "You do not have to thank me, love. When did you find out?"

"I just received a letter only a few minutes ago confirming it. Edward, I do not know what to say, I never thought that you would do anything like this for me," she pulled her hankie from her pocket to dry her eyes.

Edward, a little surprised by Naomi's comment, knew that expectant mothers were highly emotional and let it pass.

He tried to comfort her, "There, there, my love. It was my pleas—" *No, I do not want to say that. It was my duty as your husband? No.* He decided that an embrace would suffice.

Naomi sniffled, "And to think all this time I was giving Daniel all the credit."

Edward's proud smile vanished instantly. He moved Naomi away at arm's length.

"*Daniel?*" He swallowed as his face turned a bright red.

Naomi could not fathom his unexpected over-reaction. "Love, of course, I thought it was Daniel. I am sorry, but how could I possibly believe that *you* were responsible?"

In a state of fogged devastation, Edward slowly removed his hands from Naomi's shoulders.

"*Daniel?*" he repeated dropping to the divan.

"Edward, please do not be angry. Can you not see how happy I am that it was you and not Daniel—not that Daniel is incapable of such loving generosity. Mother and I were only speaking of his sweet, gentle, nature this morning."

Edward fell back limp.

Naomi knelt beside him, "Darling, are you ill? Perhaps, I should have not said anything," she fretted.

Edward *was* ill and could not speak.

"Dearest, I shan't say another word about it. Should I pay Mr. Jorgensen?"

Edward squinted up at her, "Mr. Jorgensen?" *Not him, too?* Edward rolled over in disbelief and buried his face

"I suppose that I should have told you," Naomi said regretfully.

"No, I do not want to hear this," Edward pleaded.

"I have to confess, Edward."

Edward prayed to escape this nightmare.

"Edward, I hired Mr. Jorgensen to look for Livia Nichols."

Very confused, Edward turned over and looked at her. "What?"

"I wanted to do something special for Hiram after he—"

Edward shot to his feet. "After *he* WHAT?" he demanded.

"He made me promise not to tell anyone," Naomi said remorsefully.

"I am certain that he did!" Edward said, blinded with bitterness.

"Once Hiram confessed his love for Livia, I hired Mr. Jorgensen to find her. That is how I discovered that you hired Mr. Jorgensen to find Mother. He requested payment for your case, as well." She handed Edward the letter.

Edward was thoroughly confused. He sat down and read the letter.

"Dearest, I naturally thought Daniel was responsible for bringing Mother to our wedding. I am sorry. *You* deserve all the credit." She leaned up and kissed him.

"What about the baby?" he mumbled.

"Dara? She is upstairs with Mother in the nursery. How thoughtful of you to ask."

Edward moved to the bookshelves, loathing himself for two horrific crimes: imagining Naomi's infidelity and allowing her to believe that he was responsible for Beatrice's presence at their wedding.

"Edward, now that I know, whatever inspired you to look for my mother? No one knew that she was living."

"Oh, I read it in a letter," he said without thinking.

"Letter? What letter?"

"The one from the shop clerk in Town."

Naomi stared blankly at him, processing this new information. "*You* received my letter and did not tell me?" She walked directly in front of him. "I was watching the post for weeks for that letter!"

"Now, Naomi, I wanted to surprise you," Edward gently explained, stepping back.

"All those weeks, *you* knew that my mother was alive and in London and *you* did not tell me? Edward, how could you? I trusted you and you opened my private correspondence! I am appalled, Edward McDonnally!" She stormed out of the room.

Edward stood stunned feeling as though he were the victim of a brutal cattle stampede—not once, but twice. "What about *your* opening of my letter from Mr. Jorgensen?" he called after her.

Hiram entered Brachney Hall with the innocent intention of soliciting advice of the Nettlepin Teaching Position Crisis, when he found himself caught in the crossfire.

Naomi charged forward. "Never confide in me again, Hiram McDonnally! This is all *your* fault!" She left him dumbstruck, as she marched up the stairs, wishing she had never hired Mr. Jorgensen to find Livia., even though it was after the fact.

Hiram stopped. *I knew that was coming.* He took a deep breath and continued to the library where he heard repetitive thuds. He entered cautiously to see Edward pulling books randomly from the shelves, glancing at them and dropping them to the floor.

"Edward, what are you doing?"

"Looking for a book?" Edward reported with notable anxiety.

Hiram raised his brows. "May I interrupt for a minute?"

"You are fortunate that you are still standing." Edward continued with the books.

"Aye, I met Naomi in the hall. I apologize; I should have never asked her to keep my confession discreet. You are her husband—you should have no secrets between you."

Edward turned, "*Secrets*, I am sick to death of them! Naomi came in here making me believe that I was going to be a father and the next thing I know, I am believing that Daniel, or even you are our baby's father!"

"Me? I am insulted! Edward, you are definitely confused." Hiram began retrieving the scattered books. "This is painfully reminiscent of that situation I had with Livia. Edward, trust me, these women are lacking in communication skills. It would be dangerous for them to get the right to vote." He placed two books back on the shelf. "Now, surely, you must believe that nothing happened on that day Naomi and I were at the bothy?" Hiram asked with sincerity.

"What bothy?"

Hiram stood up and swallowed hard. "You know... at Hailes Crag?" he said cautiously.

Edward dropped the book and advanced on him.

Hiram backed away, "Edward, I was tired, drunk...depressed. Nothing happened. I love Naomi—no I mean as a friend—an aunt—your wife." Hiram backed into the table. "Edward *do* not look at me that way. I have the greatest respect for your marriage to Naomi. Edward, you do not want to do this—you are no match for me."

Edward stood inches from Hiram's face and threatened, "I shall talk to you later."

Armed and ready to confront his wife, Edward left the room, knowing he was not the *only* one guilty of deception. Hiram, relieved for his uncle's departure, slid his hand across his beard, blew out, and continued picking up the books and replacing them to the shelf.

Women! Naomi, Livy, Abigail, Nettlepin, even Sophia.

"Help us Lord. Have mercy. How much can a man tolerate?"

Chapter V

"Transformation"

"Humility like darkness
reveals the Heavenly lights."

—Henry David Thoreau

Naomi sat stewing in her room, detesting the fact that her husband concealed knowledge of the letter, which had confirmed her Mother's good health and residence in London. Naomi had been deceived and in her mind, this was nearly unforgivable.

Edward mounted the stairs, agonizing over the fact that Naomi had given him grief for his misconduct while she harbored secrets of her own. She had spent some *questionable* day with Hiram, as well as, initiated an unapproved search for Livia Nichols. In Edward's opinion, these two incidents were unconscionable and unbefitting of his wife. He entered the master bedroom without introduction and closed the door. He approached Naomi who was sitting in bed with her hands folded tightly in her lap.

"Naomi, I want to speak with you," he said sternly.

"Well, I have no interest in speaking with you," she countered, refusing to look at him.

"Not interested in speaking with *me?*"

"That is exactly what I said."

"You cannot take a few minutes of your leisure time to speak with your husband, yet you can spend an entire day with my nephew?" Fuming, Edward glared down at her.

With narrowed eyes, Naomi looked up. "What ever are you ranting about?"

"You know very well," he charged.

"I have not the slightest clue."

"Should I refresh your memory?"

Naomi sat up, "Do not talk to me about memories! I lived on twelve years of memories alone of my mother, and you allowed me to continue for weeks—*unnecessary* weeks, I might add, believing that I would never see her again!"

"I wanted to surprise you. At least my secret was of an honorable basis. You on the other hand, chose to honor Hiram's wishes and keep your rendezvous secret from me! In case you have forgotten, you share the McDonnally name because you are my wife—not his!"

"Ah! How dare you insinuate that I have feelings for Hiram? I am appalled! Can I help that I am a woman of my word?" Naomi left the bed.

"You would not be in this situation if you would have stayed in Lochmoor Glen where you belong!"

"And where do you think that I have been, *Edward*?"

"Hailes Crag!"

"Hiram told you?" Naomi turned away. "Well, I do not care. I am proud that I followed him to the bothy." She faced Edward, "He may not be alive today, had I chosen not to. You should be grateful. Had you been here, *you* could have shared the responsibility."

"My nephew is a grown man; he does not need a nursemaid."

"Edward, Eloise was frantic with worry. I was the only one available. Hiram was distraught and began drinking—not because of Abigail, but his loss of Livia, years ago. I had to help him find her, I had to—I owed him!" She started to sniffle. "I left him, Edward! That night that you and I married, nearly twenty years ago, I abandoned him without so much as a single word!" Tears formed on her cheeks.

Edward watched his wife falling apart. Now, he regretted the confrontation from the moment it first began in the library. He heard her confession of guilt for his nephew, all too clearly, causing *his* guilt to resurface. The truth be known, Edward did marry Naomi out of a sense of responsibility for accidentally scarring her face with the fire poker, in the fight with her father. Nevertheless, in doing so, he had stolen Hiram's reason for living, driving him away from his home and inheritance, to a life of solitude.

Edward sat down on the bed. "You are right, Naomi. We both owe Hiram a great deal."

Naomi was silent for a minute, realizing their commonality in the situation. She wiped her eyes and sat down next to him.

"Edward, I apologize. I should have told you—not only because I am your wife, but also because Hiram is your nephew. I only wanted him to find the happiness that we have."

Edward put his arm around her. "I am sorry that I opened your letter. I had no right. But why did you not tell me about your suspicions that your mother was in Town?"

"We were planning our wedding—our real wedding. I did not want you to think that I was preoccupied with finding my mother...Edward," she lowered her gaze, "I have another confession. About Hiram, there is another reason for my feelings of guilt. I failed to introduce him to my mother at the church on our wedding day. I may have been subconsciously ignoring him and my past with him. I know it hurt him, deeply. I approached him at the reception to offer my apologies. He, of course, made light of it. I feel terrible about it. Then there is Allison; I actually accused him of courting Allison in order to punish me. Only minutes ago, I blamed him for *this* entire ordeal. With all that and Livia disappearing for years, it is no wonder that he has a raging beast inside of him. I thank God that he found Livia and I pray that she will stay with him."

Edward left the bed and turned to Naomi, "Hiram *is* unique; despite his misfortune. Between violent outbreaks, he remains charming, witty and remarkably forgiving. I do not know how he does it. He came here to speak to me and I ran him down like a steam roller."

Naomi went over and took Edward's arm, "Edward, we have to go to him. He does not deserve to be treated in this manner. We both love him dearly. He needs to know that."

Edward nodded, "I am an old hand at swallowing my pride, come on."

Naomi and Edward hurried downstairs and asked the servant who was setting the clock, "Is Hiram still here?"

"No, he left shortly after you went upstairs."

"Thank you," Edward said with disappointment.

Naomi looked at the clock. "The meeting is in a half hour. We do not have time to talk to him, now."

"We will speak to him afterwards. Until then, shall we make a pact to take care in how we address him?"

Naomi smiled in agreement.

The church was nearly filled to capacity when Hiram and Livia arrived. The McDonnally carriage paused long enough for the passengers to disembark and then returned to the manor. It was a proud moment for the couple. Hiram was ready to show off his beautiful soul mate and Livia was equally honored to be on the arm of her loving companion, one of Scotland's most respected men.

Seeing Edward chatting with his driver, Hiram suggested that Livy enter the church without him, while he spoke with his uncle. Livia agreed and Hiram cautiously approached Edward. The second Edward caught sight of Hiram, he greeted him, "Hiram, old man! Good to see you!"

Edward's fervent reception, left Hiram surprised, but pleased to find peace within the clan again.

"My dear nephew, how are you? What did you want to speak to me about at the house?" Edward asked with genuine interest.

"I am well, thank you; however, I failed to tell Livy about the unavailable teaching position."

"Not to worry, I shall handle it. Go on; join Livia. We are about ready to start."

Hiram gave a satisfied nod and did just that.

Edward and Naomi must have made amends, Hiram thought as he entered the church. He looked up to see a small girl standing in one of the pews.

"There! There is Mr. McDonnally, Auntie. Aye he is the most bonnie man in the world!" The congregation chuckled quietly.

All eyes regarded Hiram. His modesty quickly drew his focus from the girl to the floor.

"I'll be marryin' him someday," the girl stated frankly. The laughter grew louder.

Before Hiram had time to blush, a swift tug to his arm pulled him down to the pew on his left. To his great despair, it was the strike of the unrelenting Miss Nettlepin. She coiled her arm tightly around his.

Hiram looked to his captor, "Hello, Miss Nettlepin, I have—"

"I know, my dear, I have missed you too," she whispered.

I think I am going to be ill. Hiram closed his eyes. Caught in her clutches, he searched helplessly for Livy. Then he saw her, directly across the aisle from him. He felt so close, yet so far away.

Livy gave an amused, yet understanding look of approval, recognizing that his abductor was not exactly his type. The woman seated in the pew in front of Livia, turned and glared at Hiram, and then spoke to her friend.

"Aye, he is handsome enough, but I hear that his temper is horrendous."

Hiram refused to acknowledge that he heard that annoying truth. Livia did the same. Hiram faced forward trying to avoid the accommodating leach on his left. Naomi turned from the front pew, made eye contact with Hiram, and then gave a cordial little wave.

They did resolve their differences. Hiram gave her a brief nod.

Edward then took his place at the podium. "Good evening, one and all. Thank you for attending on this unusually pleasant summer's evening. As you know, we have congregated to discuss the future of the educational needs for the children of our village. Having recent charge of the Wheaton children, my wife and I are equally concerned for the reconstruction of the academic facility. Edward smiled, "Our present structure has no class and is not quite up to grade." He waited, but no one laughed at his futile attempt at humorous puns. Naomi offered a little giggle, which Edward drowned out with his serious tone.

"It is a terrible, awful, unfortunate tragedy— the burning of our school," he stammered.

Livia gave Hiram a puzzled glimpse. He dare not face her.

Edward added, "But, I am happy to report that we do have a teacher," he looked to Livy, "or two."

Hiram caught Livia's profile in his peripheral vision and grimaced at the thought of his negligence in telling her the truth of the non-existent, teaching position. Miss Nettlepin scowled, questioning Edward's "or two."

Edward made the introduction, "Tonight we are honored to have the presence of the renowned academic financial advisor and former teacher, to assist us in making our decisions. Please, welcome, Mr. Zedidah Hartstrum of London."

The men applauded, except Hiram, and the majority of the women simultaneously pulled mirrors from their purses for a final primping. Livia and Hiram observed the response with astonishment. The guest speaker took his position.

"Good evening my fellow good men and exquisite women of Lochmoor Glen. And yes, welcome children, the promise to our future and to a brighter world."

Hiram looked to the ceiling. *Get on with it.*

Zedidiah proceeded. "I will get straight to the point. I have examined your financial records and have found your coffers to be nearly empty. This would not be as unacceptable, had your school still been intact. The fact is, lovely ladies and fine gentlemen, your treasury has barely enough funds to even purchase one-third of the required desks."

The crowd moved restlessly with this report. Agnes Murray raised her hand.

"Yes, miss?"

"Hello, Mr. Hartstrum. I'm Agnes Murray. Might I suggest that we raise the funds wit' a theatrical production?"

"Miss Murray, that would be quite an undertaking."

"A musical performance—an opera o' sorts," she suggested enthusiastically. "People would come from all o'er Scotland to hear him sing."

"An *opera*?" Zedidiah snickered.

Hiram narrowed his eyes, resenting the speaker's condescension.

Agnes continued, "Aye, Hiram McDonnally bein' the leadin' actor. He has a bonnie voice. People would come from as far as London."

The residents nodded in agreement. Livy smiled proudly. Hiram remained expressionless.

Zedidiah laughed and rested his elbows on the podium. "Miss Murray, be serious. I hardly think that Mr. McDonnally's little ditties could lure in a crowd large enough to appropriate the rebuilding of the school stoop," he said with an amused smile.

The crowd gasped and slowly turned to see Hiram's response. Edward, wide-eyed, looked from Hiram, to Livy, then to Naomi. He looked back at Hiram trying to signal him discreetly, to remain calm. It was to no avail. Hiram sat for about three seconds then rose from the pew. All sat motionless as he walked down the aisle toward his offender. All that was heard was the sound of his boots hitting the floor. Miss Nettlepin's nose pointed to the rafters with pride in seeing Hiram take a stand.

"Mr. McDonnally," Zedidiah greeted.

Livia closed her eyes in quick prayer for guidance and Naomi looked fearfully to her husband, silently pleading for his intervention.

Hiram looked Zedidiah straight in the eyes.

"*Ditties?*" Hiram repeated.

"Sir, you are hardly qualified to perform for payment—to expect the public to satiate your ego with their hard-earned monies, is nothing less than unscrupulous."

Edward panicked and moved quickly to Zed's side and whispered, "I highly recommend that you retract that statement."

"No, I will do nothing of the kind. This man of extreme wealth and moderate talent, if even that, would like nothing more than to swindle these good people into destitution with his false pride and desire to be in the limelight."

Hiram was struggling; his muscles tensed, ready to react in the worst way imaginable. Livia fled from her seat and latched on to his forearm, while Edward considered hurling his body between the two men.

Livia did not hesitate. "Mr. Hartstrum."

"Yes, and who might you be, lovely one." He then grinned at Hiram. With Hiram mentally prepared to strike, Livia tightened her grip on his arm.

"My name is Livia Nichols. Despite your great financial wisdom, you failed to do your research. Mr. McDonnally is not only responsible for the construction of the first school, but he does have a tremendous voice, unless of course, you do not believe that the Metropolitan Opera is qualified to judge sufficient operatic talent."

Hiram shook his head in disapproval, "No, Livy."

Livia continued, "I am sorry, Hiram, but everyone present needs to know the truth. Mr. McDonnally was offered a position with them, less than three years ago. His choice to remain in Scotland has deterred him from accepting this offer. He is a humble man. So much so, that he has kept knowledge of this prestigious offer from all family and friends. I know this to be true, because my father had connections in the field of music." Livia turned to the residents, "Have any of you heard of this offer before today?"

Everyone replied with a headshake or a "nay." Naomi and Edward were awestruck.

Hiram relaxed and turned to face his neighbors. "We are all blessed with our individual talents. In regard to the school, you are trying desperately to stand on your own, as a community. The McDonnallys understand that you do not wish to receive our charity. That is admirable, however—"

"McDonnally—" Zedidiah cut in.

Hiram turned to face him, "Not *one* word," Hiram threatened and continued. "I will take leave of you now, but Edward would like to speak to you of a very generous proposal offered by one of our most beloved residents. My family would like to assist her in making this contribution successful. Please consider it carefully. Good evening."

The entire congregation, with exception to the perturbed Miss Nettlepin, stood and applauded as Hiram and Livia exited arm-in-arm. Miss Nettlepin refused to look at the pair.

Outside, Hiram walked toward his home with Livia at his side.

"Livy, you should not have told them. It is not important."

"I am sorry, I saw no alternative. Forgive me."

Hiram patted her arm, "How could I be angry with my greatest defender?"

"Hiram, I am aware that there is no teaching position for me."

"How did you find out?"

"Miss Nettlepin introduced herself as Lochmoor Glen's one and only teacher...and your sweetheart."

"She is unbelievable. I am sorry, I should have told you, but you had your heart set on it."

She looked at him hopefully. "It is all right, I was thinking that I could possibly open a day nursery for the little ones. I could teach them the basics."

Hiram stopped, "That is an excellent idea. I know of five or six pupils and four very tired mothers who could benefit from your school. However, I believe that Dagmar does not have an extra room available at Grimwald. Such a generous woman, to offer her home to be the site of the new school."

"My tiny school would require only a few small rooms," she looked up at him inquisitively.

"*Livy*, please, not my home."

"But you love children. You said yourself that you want a whole houseful... I suppose I could set up a tent somewhere." She lowered her head.

On its return to the church, the McDonnally carriage pulled up beside them. They climbed inside. Hiram scooted next to Livia, and placed his feet up on the opposite seat. He took her hand as the carriage pulled away.

He offered, "Three rooms in the lower west wing, but that is all. I am saving the rest for our wee McDonnallys."

Livia leaned over and hugged him, "You are positively wonderful—I love you!"

She stopped. Her face went blank, realizing that she had inadvertently said *it* for the first time. She turned to the window and eased her hand from his, regretting her lack of control. It was not what she wanted. She had hoped to hear it from him first, but now it was too late. Hiram tugged on her sleeve. Livia's flushed face turned to see his hand presenting the tiny brass passenger. Hiram moved the little toad to his ear.

"Repeat that, please," he instructed the little creature. "He says you need to repeat that last statement. He could not hear it from within my pocket."

Livia, stared down at the figurine and then avoiding Hiram's endearing gaze, she said softly, "I love you."

"You have said the magic words! *Whoosh!*" The toad disappeared to his pocket. "He has transformed into a handsome prince."

"That is not how the story goes."

"No?"

"No. A frog needs to be kissed in order to turn into a prince. And a *frog*, not a toad. "

"Oh, I forgot...hmm? We are not certain that he is a toad and not a frog." Hiram pulled the figure from his pocket and put it to her lips. She kissed it.

"*Whoosh!* He has transformed." He slid it back into his pocket. "Now is it not customary for the fair maiden to kiss the prince?"

Livia ignored him and looked out the window. Hiram's fingers guided her chin to bring her face toward his.

"Livy, my love, my only regret is that you said it first. But then, you always knew that I adored you. Livia Nichols, future mother of our six children, three daughters and three sons, a dozen dogs and one toad—I have loved you for all eternity and I promise to carry all intruding spiders safely outside...and me saying this is not at all what you desire to hear. Am I correct?"

Livy nodded.

"What you want, Livia Nichols, are three simple words, nothing more." He removed the toad from his pocket. Livia snatched it from his hand and stuffed it into her purse. Hiram placed his hand over his mouth and mimicked the muffled cry for help of his tiny captive friend.

Livia slowly removed his hand.

Hiram looked pensively down at her. It was his turn to leave the security of the "unattached."

Livia sensed his reluctance and a fearful chill ran through her as the long seconds passed.

Finally, "I love you," he whispered.

"You do?"

"I do."

"I do, too."

"I know that you do."

"I know that you do, too. Hiram, do you think that we should kiss, now?"

"Do you?"

"I do. Do you?"

"I do."

The confirming kisses lasted a mere seven minutes and forty-three seconds, ending only with the carriage's arrival at the door of Hiram's home.

Chapter VI

"The Cat's Meow"

"A sudden rush from the stairway,
A sudden raid from the hall!
By three doors left unguarded
They enter my castle wall!"

—Henry Wadsworth Longfellow

Much later that evening, the second eldest Wheaton girl, Marvel, suffering from a common eleven-year-olds appetite, tiptoed past Naomi and Edward's bedroom, to raid the pantry. She crept downstairs to the kitchen, balanced the saucer of biscuits atop a glass of milk with her right hand, and carried the oil lamp with her left. She moved gingerly down the hall to the library where she sat the lamp on the table next to her treats.

The warm glow of the flame revealed, *The Delineator*, Allison's romance magazine, on the side-table. Marvel brought the interesting periodical over to the light, flipped through the pages, and read a passage.

> *Ah! Don't struggle, Margot dearest, don't put me away, when your words, your eyes, everything, confess your love for me," he cried. "Speak! Answer me! Tell me that you are mine, mine, mine!"*

Marvel grimaced, "Ugh!" She closed the cover and tossed it back to the table. She approached the large library table noting Edward's usual layout: an assortment of neatly arranged stamps, a brass rimmed magnifying glass and the leather bound album, lying next to a variety of envelopes. Marvel munched on a biscuit while holding the magnifying lens closer to one especially large stamp. She sat the lens down and chose another biscuit.

"Hmm? Cranberries." She took a sip of milk and replaced the glass next to the stamp album. "'Tis verra bonnie," she said admiring the book which was Naomi's gift for Edward. Marvel brushed the crumbs from her fingers on her robe and carefully turned the pages. "What is that?" She lifted the lens to get a better view of an unusual stamp. "A seahorse." The words had barely passed through her lips before Dest, Naomi's kitten leapt on the table at the opposite end. "Good evenin', Dest."

The kitten mewed and began investigating. Marvel examined the stamp with further scrutiny when the kitten plunged its paw into the glass of milk.

"Dest! No!"

The kitten fearfully removed its dampened paw, but tipped the glass in the process. The remainder of the milk streamed swiftly across the pages of the priceless album.

"Oh, no!" Marvel grabbed the glass and set it aside. For lack of a cloth, she began frantically dabbing up the milk from the pages with her robe sleeve. She fervently wiped the half dozen affected pages. *This canna be happenin' to me. The McDonnallys shall skin me alive!*

First, Marvel tried blowing on the soaked pages and then resorted to fanning them. In her futile effort, she made one final attempt. Her trembling fingers held the book over the lamp's flame until her fearful eyes soon met the dried page remnants—crinkled, stained and scorched. Several stamps fluttered down to the table. Her failure at restoring the album to an acceptable condition sent her into a state of panic. She blew out the lamp and fled from the room. A second later, she returned to procure the damaged album and the telltale, loose stamps. Without hesitation, she ran into the hall and through the backdoor. She moved quickly alongside of the house to the road. With one look southward, she decided that her only alternative was to run away. *But where?* she thought. The decision was a quick one—back home to her vacant family's farmhouse.

Marvel ran until her legs ached. She stopped in front of the McDonnally mansion, knowing that it was impossible for her to continue to the farm. She walked warily up the drive and peeked in the study window to see Hiram busy at his desk. She glanced at the album and then at Hiram. She had seen him at every McDonnally gathering and several times visiting at Brachney Hall, but unlike her more outgoing siblings, Marvel had never spoken with him. Having seen his honorable behavior at the school meeting, she expected that he would advise her and treat her fairly. She tapped on the window. Hiram looked up to the gentle pecking and immediately came to the window and raised it.

"Wilmoth? It is *Wilmoth?*"

Marvel thought for a fleeting second about the unexpected opportunity to place the blame elsewhere. Her good upbringing redirected her decision. "Marvel, sir."

"Delightful name," he said, noting her robe.

"Mr. McDonnally, might I come in?"

Hiram looked suspiciously at the album in her arms. "Of course. I shall meet you at the door." He scanned the drive for a carriage and escorted her into the parlor. "Please sit down."

"Thank ya, sir. Me legs are verra tired."

"You walked from Edward's *alone* in the dark?

"I hadna choice, sir."

Hiram looked at her small hands clutching the album. "Are Edward and Naomi aware of this outing?" he asked pacing a few steps around her. Marvel shook her head. "What is troubling you, lassie?"

"Mr. McDonnally, might I confide in ya? If I wouldna promised meself to ne'er cry again, since me mother went..."

Hiram saw a single tear slip down her cheek when she held up the album at arm's length for his inspection. Hiram reached down and took it.

"Ahh...Edward's stamp album," he said solemnly.

"Aye...'tis ruined, Mr. McDonnally." Her right hand reached into her pocket. She sprinkled the stamps on the album. "Yer brother would be throwin' me to the road, so I saved 'im the trouble," she sniffled.

The impossible imagery gave Hiram a brief grin, even with the immediate sense of dread in seeing the condition of the stamps.

"Now...now, you are not going to cry—stiff upper lip... and Edward is not my brother. He, he is my uncle," Hiram stammered, accessing the damage.

Marvel looked confused. "He is?"

"Is what?" Hiram moved the brittle stamps with his index finger across the cover.

"Yer uncle?"

"Aye, my father was his older brother. I see nothing wrong with the album," Hiram said examining it.

"Inside." He flipped through the pages.

"Keep goin', sir."

"Ah...hmm?" He quirked a brow. "You spilled something on it?"

"No, sir. Not me, 'twas Dest, Mrs. McDonnally's wee kitten. He knocked o'er me glass o' milk when I was lookin' at the seahorse stamp."

"The seahorse stamp, eh." He scanned the page. "Marvel, you tried to dry them over a flame?" he shook his head with disbelief.

She nodded. Her lips began to tremble.

"Never do that again. It could have caught fire and you may have been burned." His scornful tone and dark reprimanding eyes sent Marvel to weeping, curled up at the end of the divan. Hiram stroked his beard anxiously at the pathetic sight, which he had created. He sat down next to her. He rubbed his forehead thinking, *Women! They are trained at an early age.*

"Marvel, you shan't cry," he said tenderly. "You should not have used the flame, nor should you have had a drink in such close proximity to the album. The spill *was* an accident. I am certain that you have learned your lesson and you shan't do it again," he consoled her. He offered his handkerchief. "Marvel, we need to return this to Edward and take you back to Brachney Hall before you are missed. Come along, now."

Marvel wiped her eyes, blew her nose in Hiram's handkerchief, and then handed it to him.

"Thank ya, sir. But, *please*, might I stay here," she begged pitifully.

Hiram looked uncomfortably at the soiled cloth she returned and slipped it into his pocket. "Edward and Naomi need to know that you are safe. I shall explain. They are very compassionate people."

"Tonight?"

"I shan't wake them tonight—tomorrow."

"But ye shan't be there in the morning. I shall be facin' 'em alone. I think that it is verra cold and dark now. I need to be stayin' here."

Hiram looked around the room, debating. *I cannot afford one more mistake.* He looked down at her pleading eyes, which showed him no mercy. "Very, well. You know where Sophia's room is—go on."

Marvel bounced off the divan and gave Hiram a hug and a kiss on his cheek. "Thank ya, sir."

Hiram sighed only half-believing that he had made the right decision. He ran his hand across the album. "I had better return this. Edward will panic if it is missing." Hiram turned down the hall to the secretary. He opened the center drawer and removed the duplicate key to Brachney Hall.

Several minutes later, Hiram was tying Hunter to a tree, next to the pond behind Brachney Hall. He found the backdoor still open and entered as quietly as possible, but inadvertently kicked the metal waste bin.

Upstairs, in bed, Naomi turned with a start toward her husband. "Edward, listen."

"Hmm?"

"Edward, wake up," she whispered, "there is someone breaking into the house!"

"What?" he asked, groggy and disoriented.

"Edward, it may be Cecil!"

"Cecil who?"

"Cecil—my stepbrother's father. He may still be searching for Mother!" she panicked.

"It is your overly active imagination, Naomi. It is probably, Patience."

"Edward, Patience, is lying on my feet," she pointed to her cat.

"Then it is Heidi."

"What do you think this is, lying between us?"

"Oh." He squinted at the dachshund stretched out between them on its back.

"The girls—you are putting them in danger!"

"Then give your mother to Cecil, so we can go back to sleep," he mumbled.

"Edward, that is *not* amusing."

"It may *be* your mother. Go check, Naomi."

"Edward Caleb, you *are* coming with me. Where is your sense of chivalry?"

"It is out for the night." Edward rolled over. "It may be the cook."

"Edward, she is returning tomorrow."

Naomi left the bed, peeked out the window overlooking the pond and flew back to the bed.

"Edward, Edward!" She shook him violently. He is here—I can see his horse tied by the pond!"

"What?"

"His horse—it is out there! Come see," she whispered frantically.

Edward opened one eye, slid out of bed and moved the curtain aside. He squinted in the darkness and could not deny that there was the form of a horse. "We do not know that it belongs to Cecil."

"Edward, it is an intruder, possibly a robber or murderer!"

Naomi tossed Edward his robe and pulled on hers over her nightdress. He reached to light the lamp when Naomi grabbed his wrist.

"They shall see it from the window!" Naomi warned.

Edward groaned, groped around for his slippers, and managed to put them on. Together, he and his frenzied wife tiptoed down the hall. They stepped in unison toward the staircase until they heard the sound of heavy footsteps in the hall. Edward grasped Naomi's hand.

"Edward, you have to go down alone; I have to stay with Mother and the girls," she whispered.

"Alone?"

"We cannot leave them to fend for themselves."

Edward paused and turned to Naomi. "If it happens, take the girls and Beatrice up to the ballroom. Lock the doors and send Wilmoth out to the veranda and down the trellis to get help from Hiram. Remember, I love you."

"*Wilmoth*? She is afraid of heights!"

"Then Marvel."

"Be careful, dear."

Naomi watched Edward moved stealthily down the stairs. Dest meowed. Edward put his finger to his mouth for an ineffective signal to silence the curious cat, and then continued cautiously to the umbrella stand in the hall. He carefully removed his walking stick. There was noise coming from the direction of the library. Pressed against the wall, Edward slid closer toward the dining room. He ducked inside, and then emerged slowly. Armed and ready he moved toward the library. He paused at the door aghast at the silhouette of a tall, large man hovering over the table bearing his prized album.

"Aghh!" Edward charged the figure.

Upstairs, Naomi let out a piercing scream in response to her husband's bellow. Beatrice, the dachshund, and the girls evacuated their beds and ran into the hall at record speed.

Naomi shouted, "Quick, follow Mother upstairs, I am getting Dara!"

Naomi snatched the crying infant from the basket, and was hot on the blazing trail of the three crying girls behind her mother. Naomi herded them up the steps with the aid of her barking dachshund. "Run!" she screamed when they reached the corridor. When all were safely inside the ballroom, Naomi wasted no time in sliding the key into the lock and turning it.

"Naomi, what is happening?" Beatrice demanded, out of breath.

"An intruder, Mama. Marvel, follow me." She opened the veranda doors. "Climb down quickly! Run to McDonnally Manor and get Hiram! Marvel? Marvel!" Naomi spun around. "Where is Marvel?" she asked desperately. She covered her mouth, *He may have Marvel!* Naomi quickly passed the wailing babe, toward her mother. "I have to get Hiram!"

The three trembling girls fearfully clung to Beatrice's nightgown.

"Do not worry, I will be back soon. We will find your sister!" Naomi lowered herself over the balcony and started down the trellis. When she reached the bottom, she let out a shrill cry, "AHH!"

"Naomi!" Beatrice screamed.

"Beatrice, she is fine! It is I, Edward—her husband! Everything is all right! It was Hiram! Put the children to bed and come downstairs!"

Beatrice sighed, gathering the flustered brood and the screaming infant. "There, there, it is over. We are all safe." She led them back to their beds, tucked them in and went down to speak with Naomi. Beatrice approached her daughter with concern.

"Mother, we thought that it was Cecil," Naomi explained, rubbing the stressful knots from the back of her neck.

"I thought as much. Naomi, I cannot stay here any longer. I had hoped to remain here until my cottage was built, but I will not be the cause of your living in fear of Cecil returning. I will wire Daniel tomorrow about leaving for London."

"No, Mama."

"Naomi, not to worry. I am not disappearing from your life, again. I love you. It is for the best, for now. Goodnight, Baby, I am going to bed." Beatrice kissed Naomi's forehead and continued to the stairs. Naomi joined Edward and Hiram.

"Good evening, Naomi," Hiram offered humbly.

Naomi sat down on the cobbler's bench, exhausted and replied wearily, "Hello, Hiram."

"I am sorry to cause such commotion."

"Hiram was returning my stamp album with an explanatory note." Edward moved his tongue to his cheek, and then cleared his throat to hide his disappointment in the condition of the album.

Naomi shook her head, "At this hour? I was not aware that you borrowed it."

Hiram started to leave, "I have stayed too long. I was returning it on Wilmoth's, eh... *Marvel's* behalf.

"Marvel! I forgot!" Naomi grabbed Edward's arm. "Edward, she is gone!" Naomi burst out.

"She is safe, love. Marvel is asleep in Sophia's room—temporarily hiding out. It seems that *your* kitten knocked over a glass of milk on my album and Marvel attempted to dry it over the flame of the lamp," Edward explained.

"Oh dear, she could have been burned." She sat up. "*My* kitten?" She let out a sigh and dropped back down to the bench. "Hiram I will come for her in the morning. Thank you. We apologize for your inconvenience."

"My pleasure...well, good night."

"Good night." Naomi and Edward watched him leave and returned to their bedroom.

"So much for treating Hiram with new respect, I nearly killed him down there," Edward said with remorse.

"Is he hurt badly?"

"A few ghastly bruises, no doubt."

Hiram rode home and returned Hunter to the barn. He entered his home through the backdoor and somewhat uncomfortably into Livia's arms.

"Livy, what are you doing awake?"

Livia stepped away from his reach. "I was so worried. I saw you leave. I thought that you were harboring ill feelings for Mr. Hartstrum."

Hiram threw his head back and laughed. "Come here, you bonnie lass." He pulled her in and hugged her. "I may despise the bloke, but I am not a mad man who would ride out into the night to hunt him down."

"Where did you go?"

"On a mission of mercy that resulted in utter chaos and my near death."

"*Hiram?*" she frowned with concern.

"Aye, my love, take heed. Never, and I mean *never*, enter Brachney Hall at night, unannounced—especially if you have Edward's cherished stamp album in your possession."

Livia looked up at him, confused. Hiram leaned down and pointed to his crown. She separated his shiny black curls with her fingers.

"Uh," he moaned.

"Who did this to you?"

He looked up and kissed her.

"Livy, if you are to become a member of this clan, you need to become accustomed to the bizarre and unexpected. I will explain tomorrow."

Chapter VII

"Negotiations"

"She saw a rider draw his rein
And gazing down with timid grace,
She felt his pleased eyes
Read her face."

—John Greenleaf Whittier

After four days, traversing the North Sea, Rahzvon and friends had assembled on deck to view the Norwegian coastline. They spent the last evening discussing the arduous route through the Trollhiemen Mountains to the tiny country of Kosdrev. After leaving the ship, they would eat at the port inn before hiring a carriage to take them to the small cottage owned by Rahzvon's aunt, Lillitheen, near the Kosdreven border.

The inn's specialty, chicken stew and cornbread, satisfied their hearty appetites before they gathered in an alcove off the main dining room to discuss the details of Rahzvon's plan. Rahzvon spoke quietly to avoid unwanted eavesdropping of potentially dangerous patrons. However, after only a minute, Rahzvon detected an intruder encroaching on their privacy. The small, gray-bearded man had left his table from across the room and moved adjacent to the alcove. Rahzvon immediately moved his party outside, behind the inn, to a small table where the employees took tea. After double-checking for lurking strangers, Rahzvon continued.

"Sven, an associate of my father, is delivering the horses and provisions to my aunt's home. Our destination is a vault in a passageway beneath the castle." Trina and Allison looked worriedly at one another, while Sophia's face lit up with her usual sense of adventure.

Rahzvon explained, "My fortune awaits in this vault. Until this moment, only my father and I had knowledge of its existence. Early on, my father was weary of the astute Princess Creazna and suspected that she could never be trusted. Thus, he built the vault. I have never seen it."

"How are we to find it?" Sophia inquired.

"Before my father was executed, he revealed the location of the key and a map depicting its position in the tunnel."

"Do we have to enter the castle in order to get into the passageway?" Trina asked apprehensively.

"Excellent question. The answer is *no*, as there is another entrance beneath an abandoned shed in the woods, east of the castle."

"How can you be certain that no one has discovered the vault?" Guillaume asked.

"Or is livin' in the shed?" Tavy added.

"I have no way of knowing, either. However, it is highly improbable that anyone found the vault. The tunnel, formerly an escape route for the royal family in time of an attack, is lined with rock. The vault is hidden behind one of them." Rahzvon looked deep into the eyes of his followers. "I need not remind you that I am not welcome in Kosdrev— neither are my companions. We shall have to move stealthily and quickly. I beg you, now, to reconsider. I can do this on my own."

"Would it not be beneficial to have the advantage of many watchful eyes?" Trina asked.

"It would, but I do not relish the idea of your capture by the merciless Creazna."

"This wench, Creazna, darena touch a hair on any o' yer heads," Tavy threatened.

"If we still have them." Guillaume gulped.

"Zigmann, your honor is not at stake here. You may remain behind to protect the women?" Rahzvon offered.

"Behind? We are going," Sophia refuted.

Ignoring Sophia's objection, Rahzvon explained, "My aunt has no idea of my plan to return to Kosdrev. She thinks I am on holiday, hiking in the mountains. I prefer her ignorance of the matter to insure her safety. Sven will provide us with Kosdreven attire. In the event that we are seen, if we are dressed like the locals, we will not raise suspicion, because in Kosdrev tourism is unheard of. Now, it is getting late and we need to hire a carriage." Rahzvon led his troupe to the livery stable.

"Rahzvon, we are going, too!" Sophia chased after him.

After a short-lived row between Rahzvon and Sophia, which ended abruptly at Rahzvon's command, the group rode silently to Lillitheen's home.

"*Tuanym* Lillitheen!" Rahzvon called out to the rotund woman waving in the doorway of the gray stone cottage.

"Rahzvon, *veimyo shaised!*"

"I, too," he replied embracing her and kissing her cheek. "These are my very dear friends, Allison, Trina, Guillaume, McTavish—*Tavy*, and," he put his arm around Sophia, "Phia."

"A handsome group, Rahzvon. Welcome, all of you. Come in, come in." Lillitheen held the door for the guests as they filed past her.

"I hope you do not mind a few more houseguests," Rahzvon commented after shooting a look of warning to Sophia, openly brooding over Rahzvon's intention to leave the women at the cottage.

"My cats and I welcome all of you, *noelvedo.*" Lillitheen leaned down to pet a large, white, long-haired feline, rubbing against her leg.

"Rahzvon squatted down and stroked the cat, "Hello Callitil. *Tuanym*, did you enjoy your visit to

England?" Rahzvon asked taking a seat next to Sophia on the hearth bench.

His aunt picked up the cat and walked to the window. "It was quite pleasurable, but I missed my mountain."

Allison joined her. "Such a beautiful view."

"Beautiful it is, from a safe distance. Deadly if one trespasses too closely," she said stroking her cat.

All looked uncomfortably to the window.

"My uncle, fell from the mountain, ten years ago," Rahzvon explained, leaving the bench to place a comforting arm over his aunt's shoulders.

"My Argyn was a good man. The entire world suffered a loss with his passing. Come now, I shall prepare you something to drink," Lillitheen offered.

Over tea, Rahzvon's aunt and Allison exchanged cat tales. Allison spoke of her mother's cat, Patience, and its miraculous return from the dead with the tiny kitten, Dest. Lillitheen recounted the story of Callitil guiding her to her fallen husband, allowing her to share his last few minutes. Guillaume proudly reported the antics of his clever dachshund, and Tavy joined in with a story of a sea dog that saved him from drowning.

Rahzvon, disturbed with Sophia's silence led her outside with the excuse to show her the rock garden. "Phia, your silence is rude and intolerable."

Sophia looked at the night sky without comment.

"My aunt does not deserve this behavior from one of her guests. You can continue to pout, out here, or you can put a smile on your face and join me inside," Rahzvon said impatiently.

Sophia looked to see the anger blazing in his glare and followed him in.

Lillitheen offered Sophia the rocking chair and requested, "Rahzvon, play for us. Give your old aunt a moment to treasure. It has been such a long time." Rahzvon looked around at his interested friends, then to the curious Sophia.

"Go ahead, *noelvedo*, do not keep me waiting." Lillitheen smiled resuming her place next to Sophia.

Rahzvon walked over to the corner of the room and lit the wall lamp. He opened a brocade cloth sack, revealing the magnificently carved buckhorn. Trina and Allison gasped at the sight of the beautiful instrument. Sophia raised her brows with surprise.

"I gave it to my Argyn for a wedding gift. He taught Rahzvon to play as a boy, when he visited on holiday from Kosdrev. It was not long before he could play as well as his uncle."

Rahzvon sat down, staring at the horn, then Sophia. He positioned his mouth and began. The melancholy music filled the cottage and soon brought tears to the women. Tavy and Guillaume observed respectfully, astonished that their large friend could produce such heart-wrenching sounds.

When Rahzvon reached the finale, his aunt wiped her eyes with her handkerchief, while the others applauded his efforts and rushed over to congratulate him. Sophia sat awestruck having witnessed yet another unknown talent of the man she loved. Rahzvon immediately addressed her.

"Phia, did you not like my playing?"

To everyone's surprise, Sophia ran outside. Rahzvon followed her and found her crying at the edge of the road.

"*Phia*," he said compassionately.

"Why did you not tell me?"

"That you were not going with us?"

"No, that you had musical talent," she said trying to control her sobs.

"*Musical talent?* I never thought that it was important."

"I feel that I do not know you."

He put his arms around her. "Trust me, Phia, you know me better than anyone and sometimes I believe that you know me better than I know myself. Come on, it is cold out here. We all need to get some sleep."

Lillitheen showed the women to their room and then directed the men to theirs. Guillaume gave Allison a gentle hand squeeze as he retired, while Tavy winked at Trina. Lillitheen gave Sophia a hug and Rahzvon a kiss on the cheek.

"You have made an excellent choice, Rahzvon. I can see the love in your eyes for this little one. Good night children."

Rahzvon stood in the hall alone with Sophia.

"She is a lovely woman, Rahzvon. I am glad that I met her."

"Yes, she has been very good to me. She is the closest I have to a mother. Now, *Little One,* sleep well." They shared a discreet kiss before returning to their rooms.

"See you in the morning," Rahzvon said closing the door behind him.

Their next few days were spent at the cottage, reminiscing with Lillitheen, and exploring the grounds of her estate. Rahzvon felt obligated to share some time with his hospitable aunt who rarely had the pleasure of visitors. One night before turning in, Sophia detected that Rahzvon's kiss was unusually passionate. Then with his eyes intensely focused on hers, he whispered *Leslew zaward skichared,* as his hand slipped from hers. Sophia watched him close the door without his usual phrase regarding the next morning.

I do know you. You are planning to leave without me, before morning, Sophia suspected. She rushed in to relay her suspicions to her roommates.

Meanwhile, Rahzvon addressed Guillaume and Tavy in a low tone. "We are leaving tonight, without the women."

"They are going to be angry," Guillaume whispered. Tavy shrugged with indifference.

"Yes, but they will be safe," Rahzvon replied rummaging through the bureau drawers. "Those clothes should be here, somewhere. Ah, here they are." He opened a crate in the corner.

Tavy and Guillaume looked inquisitively at the Kosdreven apparel as Rahzvon pulled it out. Rahzvon handed Guillaume a dark green wool top.

"I think that I shall look like Robin Hood," Guillaume said admiring the felt jacket.

"*Zigmann,*" Rahzvon said annoyed.

"Sorry."

"Hurry and put these on." Rahzvon tossed a leather jacket to Tavy.

"Verra interestin'," Tavy remarked, slipping it over his shirt.

"I *do* look like Robin Hood," Guillaume said with admiration before the bureau mirror. Tavy shook his head.

Rahzvon whispered, "Well, come along my merry men." Guillaume headed for the door.

"No Zigmann, too risky—out the window," Rahzvon instructed.

The three men crept out behind the cottage and around to the barn.

"The horses are inside," Rahzvon slowly pulled the door open.

"For men, you took an awfully long time to dress," Sophia said, outfitted in riding apparel from her head down to her *ugly* boots. She sat astride one of the three horses.

Seeing all three women seated atop *their* horses, Rahzvon put his hands on his hips and turned to his male followers, giving them a "now what?" look. He turned back to Sophia.

"I said *no*, Phia. Absolutely not." He shook his head. "Dismount, all of you."

"Stand united, women," Sophia announced. "Er…sit united."

Rahzvon turned to Tavy and Guillaume, "All right men, let's take them down," he motioned them to follow his lead.

"Halt, Mr. Sierzik! If you so much as lay a finger on me, I shall never allow you to kiss me again," Sophia proclaimed.

Rahzvon stopped, thought for a minute and grinned. "You know that you cannot possibly honor that threat."

"I certainly can and I shall."

"Phia, you are in danger as it is. Creazna despises me. If she finds that you are here, she will send her minions out after you—after all of you. The border between the countries does not guarantee your safety. At least, by remaining here, Sven will have time to get you to safety, if something goes wrong. Is it not enough that my aunt's life and home are in jeopardy? Now, please, be reasonable. Get down."

"We came this far and we are staying together." Sophia sat straight in the saddle.

"So you prefer to die with me?" Rahzvon muttered as he moved in and took a hold of the bridle of Sophia's horse.

"If need be."

Guillaume cringed at the mere mention of the grave danger.

"Do you see any more horses, Phia?" Rahzvon asked angrily.

"Climb aboard. These horses are big. They can handle two riders," Sophia said sharply.

"Phia, take a good long look at your opponents here. Do you honestly believe that the three of you are a match for us?" Rahzvon looked to Guillaume who attempted an intimidating stance with his hands on his hips, and then to Tavy, who stood tall with his arms folded across his chest.

"Guillaume, you look like Robin Hood," Allison commented.

"I do?" he smiled proudly, straightening the hem of his shirt.

Rahzvon rolled his eyes.

Sophia sat firm, "We have rights as women. In Finland, women have had the vote for nearly eight years and for twenty-one in New Zealand. Are they any better than us?"

"Vote? The women of Kosdrev are not allowed on the streets before sunrise or after sunset. However, here in Norway they were granted the vote last year...Very well, I concede. You may go with us," Rahzvon agreed.

Sophia smiled victoriously. Allison and Trina looked skeptically at the men.

"Mount up men. Guillaume, you ride with Sophia, McTavish, you with Allison and I shall ride with Trina," Rahzvon directed.

Guillaume hesitated, not pleased with the orders positioning Tavy with *his* Allison,

Sophia objected immediately. "Why are you riding with Trina?"

Rahzvon replied in a controlled tone, "Because Trina barely knows McTavish and she definitely would be uncomfortable riding with Guillaume...considering their past."

"Trina does not know *you,* either*!*" Sophia protested.

"Phia, Trina and I sat together at Naomi and Edward's wedding. Remember?" Rahzvon taunted, while approaching Trina's horse.

Sophia panicked and quickly dismounted. "No, I can ride with Trina!"

"Then I shall ride with Allison," Rahzvon walked toward Allison.

"No! Guillaume can ride with Allison," Sophia suggested.

"My dear, who am I to ride with?" He looked questionably at McTavish.

"Oh," Sophia realized that her arrangements failed miserably.

Rahzvon moved swiftly to the empty saddle on Sophia's horse and mounted. Before Sophia had time to react, Tavy was standing next to Trina motioning for her to climb down.

"It is no use, Sophia," Allison slipped from the saddle with Guillaume's assistance. Trina followed suit.

Sophia glared at Rahzvon, "If you leave, we shall find more horses and follow you!"

That remark did not set well with Rahzvon. He climbed down, took a hold of Sophia's hand and led her swiftly from the barn.

"Phia, have you ever noticed how many times that you have forced me to take you aside to speak privately with you?" he asked in frustration.

"Forced?" Sophia jerked her hand from his. "How dare you speak with me with such condensa..."

"Condescension? Be angry, be furious, I do not care. You are going to promise me that you will not follow us, or I shall never return to Scotland."

Sophia recognized this as one of Rahzvon's serious, do-not-tempt-me moments. She had no choice. She clenched her fists and stomped the ground with anger befitting Hiram McDonnally's niece.

"Are you quite finished?" Rahzvon asked. Sophia looked away.

"I will return in a few days, Phia, and then we shall go home to Lochmoor Glen, together."

Sophia looked to the ground. He placed his fingers under her chin and raised it.

"Little One, give me a smile to take with me. Sophia Sierzik is a beautiful name. Do you not agree?" Sophia tightened her lips, fighting her tears. "Phia, it is time. Gather your friends and return to the cottage."

Rahzvon led her back into the barn where Sophia saw Trina placing something in Tavy's hand.

Sophia tugged on Rahzvon's sleeve. "*Bosiw ed guth,*" she whispered and darted away to the cottage. Trina and Allison scurried after her while the three men walked their horses out of the barn, tightened their cinches and mounted.

"How did you convince her?" Guillaume asked Rahzvon.

"It is unimportant. Let's go. The sooner we get back, the better."

The women returned to their room and sat silently on their beds.

Finally, Trina asked Sophia, "Are we going to get horses and follow them?"

"No, or I shall remain a McDonnally forever."

"Sophia, what did you say to Rahzvon, before you left?" Trina asked.

"May the Almighty assist you. What did you give Tavy?"

"Something for good luck—I really do not believe in such things, but being a sailor—he does."

"I wish that I would have given Rahzvon something to take with him," Sophia lamented.

Allison moved over beside her.

"Sophia, Rahzvon does not need a token, he has your love."

Sophia gave a brief smile, fell back to the pillow and stared at the ceiling.

Sophia Sierzik, yes it is beautiful.

"But this was my father's faith
I suffered chains and courted death;
That father perished at the stake
For tenets he would not forsake;"

—Lord Byron

Chapter VIII

"Devlin"

"All in the dark we grope along,
And if we go amiss
We learn at least which path is wrong,
And there is gain in this."

—Ella Wheeler Wilcox

Across the sea, many miles from Lochmoor Glen, Rahzvon, Guillaume and Tavy, relying on their sure-footed horses moved cautiously through the unfamiliar terrain. The cold night air of the higher altitude cut through their Kosdreven outerwear with razor sharpness.

"Rahzvon!" Guillaume summoned.

"Quiet!" Rahzvon halted his horse. "Zigmann, do not address me with my given name. It is known all too well, here."

"What shall I call you?"

"Aye, gypsy, what name do ya prefer?" Tavy taunted,

"Uh...Marcus."

"I could be Robin," Guillaume chimed in.

"*Zigmann*, no one knows you here. There is no need to change yours." Rahzvon kicked his horse to move it forward.

Guillaume moved up quickly beside him. "Are you certain?" he asked, disappointed.

"Yes, now keep moving. I want to get to the forest as quickly as possible. Why were you calling me?"

"I forgot."

Rahzvon shook his head.

It was slow going on the moonlit path. The troupe edged forward.

"We shall stop ahead, to water the horses at the stream," Rahzvon announced.

After they dismounted and led their horses down to the water, Guillaume began gathering sticks and placed them in the clearing, about thirty feet away.

"What are ya doin'?" Tavy asked.

"I am about to prepare the most structurally

efficient fire that you have ever seen."

Rahzvon stepped over and kicked the pile aside, "Zigmann, there will be no fire. We cannot risk drawing the attention of my adversaries."

Guillaume looked down at his decimated pile and then cupped his hands and began blowing on them to warm them. Rahzvon slid down in the dirt next to a boulder.

"Please, sit down. We need to discuss some things." Guillaume sat across from him cross-legged; Tavy sat with out-stretched legs. Rahzvon picked up a handful of dirt and let it fall through his fingers.

"If I am captured, do not risk your necks to help me. Get out and get the women out of the country. In the event that either of you are taken prisoner, do not reveal your association with me. The empire may be ruthless, but it is not in the habit of executing outsiders. You may create whatever story you see fit, as long as you do not mention my name or my father's. Sven is serving as our reconnaissance. If I am taken captive, he has been instructed to alert my allies within the palace and then return to vacate my aunt and the women." He stood up, "The palace is relatively quiet by this hour. Unfortunately, Sven informed me that the number of guards has been doubled on the perimeter."

"Are they aware that you are returning, Rahzvon—I mean Marcus?" Guillaume asked.

"No. It seems that Creazna has a revolution brewing in her kingdom. It began with the execution of an elder of the Church."

"Why? Was he refusin' to marry her, too?" Tavy offered cynically, as he turned over Trina's token several times.

"Good guess. He refused to officiate at her wedding to Alanvahs of Devlin...on moral grounds."

"*Devlin?* That has a foreboding ring to it," Guillaume stood up and brushed the dirt from his pants.

Rahzvon looked toward the north, "It should— it is a barbaric kingdom situated north of Kosdrev. This union between the two kingdoms would be disastrous for my people. They would as soon migrate and starve, before they would honor Alanvahs' ruling."

"What do ye plan to do about it, *Marcus?*" Tavy asked.

"About what?"

"The revolution and savin' *yer* people."

"It is no longer my country, or my battle, McTavish." Rahzvon glared at him. "There is nothing that I can do—I am but one man."

"Nay, yer but three," Tavy corrected.

"And how do you propose that we aid their efforts?" Rahzvon scoffed.

Tavy stood up. "Overthrow the royal court."

"McTavish, you are mad." Rahzvon walked over to the stream and untied his horse.

"'Tis not me country and I would be willin' to help." He raised a brow in an inquiring glance directed to Rahzvon, before walking his horse to the clearing.

Guillaume listened nervously, with his arms folded and his hands tucked under his armpits.

Rahzvon took a drink from his water flask, "You are out of your head, McTavish."

"I agree," Guillaume added, leading his horse from the stream.

"How many allies would there be waitin' inside?" Tavy persisted.

"Only nine and that gives us a total of twelve to fight off over two-hundred foot soldiers. No more about it." Rahzvon tightened his cinch.

"I think need we to be devisin' a plan to end the marriage," Tavy tapped his steepled fingers to his lips.

"How?" Guillaume asked.

"No man wants to be made the fool by a woman. I may be getting' meself captured," Tavy boasted.

"You will do nothing of the kind. McTavish, your overactive ego will inevitably be cause for your demise, but not under my watch." Rahzvon climbed into the saddle and gave the cinch one more tug.

"Other than, *Sophia*," Tavy pointed out, "I've yet to meet a lassie who can resist a seafarin' Scotsman...It shan't take much. I shall be captured while yer retrievin' yer fortune. Before the night is o'er, word will be known to the king of Devlin, that his Princess' eyes hae wandered to the west. Rumor has been the ruin o' many a couple," Tavy said confidently.

"McTavish, come back to reality and mount up. Do you actually believe that I would put the fate of Kosdrev in the hands of one arrogant sailor? You stay out of trouble. If anything were to happen to you, Phia would never—" Rahzvon stopped short.

"Ne'er *what*?" Tavy grinned, pleased.

"For Trina's sake, McTavish—Trina's, not Sophia's." Rahzvon snapped the reins and Guillaume and Tavy mounted and followed.

Rahzvon stopped his horse on the crag overlooking the silhouette of the palace against the night sky. He viewed it with mixed emotions. It was his birthplace and childhood home, yet it was the scene of his father's unjust death.

Tavy sensed Rahzvon's discomfort and rode up beside him. "After me father was lost at sea, in the thrill o' settin' sail, his face flashed before me eyes. I would begin searchin' the waters for him, like a madman." He reached down and patted his horse's neck. "The pain is to be expected."

Rahzvon turned and gave Tavy an appreciative nod and led the way easterly along the ridge. Rahzvon stopped again to get his bearings. The clouds drifted beyond the moon, presenting a clear picture of the medieval structure below.

Guillaume shuddered. "It looks like something out of a horror story."

Rahzvon turned in his saddle, "It is much worse inside."

Guillaume gulped. To his delight, the temperature rose as they descended to the valley below. Soon the depths of the Rebandyn Tog Forest surrounded the three riders.

At Lillitheen's cottage, a carriage appeared. Rahzvon's aunt stirred momentarily and went to back to sleep. A figure quietly disembarked, went directly to the back of the house, and stole around to the window of the girls' bedroom. He tapped lightly at the pane.

Allison awoke first and shook Sophia. "Wake up, there is someone at the window," she whispered.

Sophia and Allison peeked beyond the curtain to see the strange man.

"My name is Sven—a friend of Rahzvon."

"How can we be sure?" Sophia asked.

"Rahzvon asked that I supply him with three horses and provisions. Were they not in the barn?"

"Yes...why do you awaken us? Is Rahzvon in trouble?" Sophia asked anxiously.

"Rahzvon is very well. In fact, to his surprise, he was well-received and asked that I bring you three ladies to meet with him at the palace," he reported cheerily.

"He asked for you to come for us, tonight?" Allison asked tilting her head.

"Yes, he said that he missed his woman."

Sophia smiled proudly. "We need to dress!"

"I shall be waiting for you in the carriage."

Sophia hopped on the bed to wake Trina. "Trina, we are going to the palace. Rahzvon has sent for us."

Trina opened her eyes and squinted. "Are you certain?"

"Yes, now make haste. Sven is waiting," Sophia insisted while changing her clothing.

The carriage pulled away with Sven and the three women inside. Sophia was elated with the thought of seeing Rahzvon within hours, Trina was a little nervous about seeing Tavy, and Allison, the eldest of the three, was leery of the unexpected arrangement. This late night development tugged skeptically at her intuitive fears.

No sooner had Allison's instincts screamed disaster, when Sven displayed his pistol.

"You are fools—like all women," he mocked.

"Where are you taking us and where is Rahzvon?" Sophia demanded.

"Rahzvon should be taken into custody within the hour and you my lovely, ignorant ladies will be sold at the slave market in Devlin. Do not worry, you shall bring a fair price," he laughed.

"You beggarpig!" Sophia denounced.

"I knew it," Allison mumbled.

"You, sir, shall never escape Tavy's revenge!"

Trina blurted out shaking her fist.

Sophia and Allison looked at her with a little surprise, and then nodded in agreement.

"Rahzvon's too!" Sophia added.

Sophia and Trina looked immediately to Allison for her input. She gave a quick headshake, doubting Guillaume's chivalric instincts.

All three women began firing a barrage of complaints to their kidnapper. Sven, *their* captured audience, shook his pistol at them and threatened all three to either be quiet or he would be delighted to gag them.

The carriage rattled along through the night with bits of starlight lighting Sven's vengeful grin. After Rahzvon's banishment, Sven, unfortunately, had become the object of Creazna's wrath. His only chance for survival was to carry out the princess' orders to prove his worthiness as a loyal subject. Tonight would guarantee his longevity.

The atmosphere of the carriage was intense as the three, duped passengers devised their individual plans of escape. Sven sat relaxed with ultimate control: the threat of his firearm. Sophia glanced at Allison, Allison at Trina. Trina raised the back of her hand to her forehead.

"I am feeling ill," she whined, closing her eyes.

"Motion sickness again, Trina?" Sophia asked sympathetically.

Sven was immediately disturbed at the thought of witnessing Trina lose her supper.

"I feel faint," Trina warned.

"It is the boots! They are too tight!" Sophia looked to Trina's feet—as did Sven. She leaned down to untie them.

"No, no!" Allison exclaimed, sitting on Trina's left. "She needs air, we had better hurry!"

"Hurry, it is coming!" Trina screamed and cupped her hands at her mouth.

Sven's attention darted from Allison struggling at the window—to Sophia, fighting with the shoelaces, back to Trina now gagging and holding her stomach.

"No, no, it is—" Sophia yelled and all three dove at their captor, knocking the gun from his hand. Allison quickly retrieved it from the floor in the scuffle.

"I have it!" she announced, firmly holding the gun in her hand. Sophia and Trina returned to their seats.

"Give it to me," Sven said coolly. "That is a dangerous weapon."

"Not one more word. I am not interested in your opinions," Allison warned. "Ladies, remove your bootlaces and tie his wrists and ankles. Tie his hands behind him. No quick movements. Trina, take my scarf and gag him with it. Sven, I believe that was *your* idea. We thank you."

The three women sat back satisfied, as their prisoner lay hunched over, in the seat across from them. Although basking, momentarily, in their victory, they dreaded the thought of their possible destination, coupled with the impossibility of walking poised in their laceless, ugly boots.

When the castle came into view, Sophia whispered, "Now." The three pushed him from the carriage and Sven became a part of the landscape, with the driver being none the wiser.

As they moved beneath the trees, Guillaume addressed Rahzvon, "I now remember what I was going to ask. What if this building, with the secret entrance, is demolished, Marcus?"

"As I told Trina, earlier, we will have to use the known entrance to the passageway."

"Would that be dangerous?" Guillaume shifted uneasily in his saddle.

"Very."

Guillaume swallowed and lowered his head, praying that the shack would be there.

Remembering the details of the map, Rahzvon navigated his way to the site, aided by the familiar landmarks—the stream, the two tree trunks wound together with vines and lastly the pile of stones generated in the clearing by the shack, which was an abandoned outpost for the guards. In seeing the small, dilapidated building, Rahzvon encouraged his horse to quicken its pace to an area south. He instructed Tavy and Guillaume to remain behind while he investigated. He slid below the single window in the back and peeked inside. It was black as pitch and he could see nothing. He removed his flashlight and approached the door. Opening it slowly, he shot the beam around the room. A single rat darted through a hole to escape the bright light. He shone the light to the planks on the floor. Just as his father had noted—the floor was designed in quarter sections to disguise the break for the trapdoor.

"Thank you, Mr. Hubert," Rahzvon mumbled with gratitude for the invention of the portable torch. He stepped outside, surveyed the area, and signaled for Guillaume and Tavy to join him. They tied their horses and walked over to the building.

"This is it and that corner panel on the upper far left is the trapdoor to the tunnel."

"A bit wee for me body," Tavy complained.

"You are no bigger than I, McTavish," Rahzvon replied, annoyed with Tavy's arrogance. "Hold this,

Zigmann." Rahzvon handed Guillaume the light while he slid his fingers along the wall, in search of the lever to lift the panel. Rahzvon discovered it midway, pushed on it and jammed his hand under the outer edge to raise the panel.

"McTavish might be right," Guillaume suggested, considering the small opening. "I am not sure either one of you will fit through there."

"You had better hope that we can," Rahzvon grinned, "or you will be the chosen one."

Guillaume stepped back anxiously.

"We are going down, Zigmann. Take the horses and tie them behind the hill. It is about a quarter mile. Then come back and stand guard, keeping the panel closed. Make haste!"

Guillaume hesitated.

"*Zigmann?*" Rahzvon placed his hands on his hips, perturbed with his delay.

"Marcus, if I die, tell Allison that I loved her."

"Zigmann, you are not going to die, but I shall tell her. Now, go!"

"Wait! Tell her that I was going to ask her to marry me."

Tavy grinned. Rahzvon nodded as he dropped into the hole.

"And tell her that I had a ring for her," he told Tavy as he lowered himself down.

"Aye, be goin', now." Tavy started to close the trapdoor when Guillaume shot back and knelt at the opening.

"Please remind her to take Rusty for his walks, he will miss them."

Tavy rolled his eyes and lowered the panel.

Guillaume left to hide the horses while Rahzvon and Tavy began their trek through the winding tunnel. Neither man spoke as they moved wide-eyed, prepared at every turn for the presence of the unexpected. Unfortunately, the splashing of their footsteps in the underground stream echoed throughout the passageway. They moved closer to the walls, avoiding contact with the water.

Guillaume's heartfelt memos left Rahzvon unsettled, with hampering thoughts of Sophia. She was everything that he wanted—beautiful, intelligent, adventuresome, creative and strong-willed. Although, these traits had often served as irritants for him, on one occasion or another, overall, they made Sophia the woman she was—the woman for whom he would risk his life. He could not imagine, not seeing her again.

Tavy, like Rahzvon, trod along with Trina's token held tightly in his fist. He, too, considered the importance of Trina's presence in his life. She was unlike the few women whom he had courted—in her social standing, her mannerisms, and more importantly, in her genuine interest in him. He imagined returning with her to Scotland and lamenting the day that he would be going out to sea and leaving her behind. For the first time, he felt that there actually might be more to life than fishing.

Chapter IX

"The Architect"

"All architects of Fate
Working in these walls of time
Some with massive deeds and great,
Some with ornaments with rhyme"

—Henry W. Longfellow

Guillaume watched and waited, calm and collected, at his post at the shack. His thoughts of amour inspired him to design the first home that he would build for Allison. It would have a sunny breakfast room and a special dressing room to accommodate her many beautiful frocks. Muffled conversation outside brought him to his feet. Guillaume opened the door slowly and stepped outside.

"*Gohow sereth?*" the man called out from the darkness.

Guillaume assumed it was an inquiry to his identification and replied, "My name is...Robin— Robin Zigmann."

Two uniformed men appeared, walking their horses. "An Englishman."

"Actually, my father was born in Germany and my mother is part French and part German."

The two men looked at one another curiously to Guillaume's unconventional reply.

"What are you doing here?"

"I am an architect."

"An architect?" Skeptical, the shorter man looked up at his taller comrade and whispered, "*Betoi ud.*"

Guillaume quickly spoke up, "Yes, I am touring the world—observing examples of archaic...architecture. This small structure is the perfect example of the very primitive design—*une porte, une fenêtre.* Translation? One door, one window," Guillaume explained in an authoritative tone.

"You came across the sea from Britain to study this?" The shorter men squinted skeptically.

"No, this and the castle. Everyone has heard of the magnificent Castle of Kosdrev and the

Princess Creazna," Guillaume smiled. That benevolent description of the palace immediately raised suspicion with the soldiers.

"Is the Princess aware, Mr. *Robin* Zigmann, that you are wandering about her kingdom?"

"I can honestly say that she is definitely responsible for me being here," Guillaume assured them. The two men exchanged grins and nodded.

"Come with us."

Guillaume backed up to the door. "There is nothing that I would enjoy more than laughing about old times with the Princess over a spot of tea. One minute, please. Uh...might I fetch my equipment—*tools of my trade*. My bag is inside." Guillaume closed the door, darted to the window, raised the sash, hit the trapdoor lever and disappeared beneath it.

The taller man commented, "Hmm? Sierzik's man? Is it possible?" he snickered. He turned and started toward the shack. "Make haste in there!

As there was no reply, the two men then entered the empty shack shouting furiously, peering out of the window. They ran outside in search of their missing prisoner whose departure verified his alliance with Rahzvon.

Guillaume waited under the trapdoor until any evidence of his pursuers had vanished. He peeked beneath the panel. He was safely alone. *Marcus and Tavy must have been captured!* With this belief, Guillaume realized that it was now his responsibility to come to their rescue. He ran for his horse and rode back to the ridge.

In the meantime, Rahzvon and Tavy moved through the passageway until Rahzvon's light fell on the two large stones with the white vertical lines, described on Gaelon's map. Rahzvon pulled the folded paper from his pocket for verification.

"There they are," he pointed to the sketch.

"Aye, shall we pull'em out?"

"Yes, and quickly." They removed their knives and chiseled around the stones to allow adequate room for their fingers. Together they pulled out the first one, revealing a space leading to the main tunnel. Then they removed the second, producing a hole barely large enough for their entry.

"My father was a much smaller man," Rahzvon explained as Tavy shimmied through to join him on the other side.

"He ne'er expected his son to be such a strappin' lad, eh?" Tavy joked as he stood up and brushed himself off.

"I suppose not." They replaced the stones back into the hole.

"What ye say we dunna forget where these are located?"

Rahzvon smiled and flashed the light to the winding passage to the right. "That is the escape exit for the royal family."

He directed the light to a sharp bend to the right, ahead. They rounded the corner.

"Halt!"

Their hearts stopped. It was over. Princess Creazna and two dozen armed foot soldiers stood before them. Another ten moved in from behind them.

"*Veimyo shaised*, Rahzvon Sierzik."

Rahzvon fought from speaking the disdainful words that filled his head.

"Down on your knees! You are in my kingdom!" she demanded.

Rahzvon's animosity for his father's murderess prevented his compliance. However, Tavy's desire to remain in her good graces, as to initiate his plan, respectfully dropped to his knees and lowered his head. Rahzvon observed Tavy's submission and did the same, only as insurance to protect his friend.

"You may rise," she said staring at Tavy. "Who is this man?"

"A comrade," Tavy replied.

"A comrade?" she looked him over with great interest.

"Yer Highness, Henry McTavish, sailor o' Scotland, at yer service," Tavy bowed.

Rahzvon rolled his eyes.

She walked around him admiring his musculature, "A Scot...and a sailor, too," she said, obviously impressed.

Tavy winked at his astonished friend, as the princess walked back to her guards.

She smirked, and then reported, "Sven Yagdub tells me that you have returned for your inheritance."

Rahzvon clenched his teeth. *Sven, that—*"I have."

"I know of no such monies," she said crossly.

"I said nothing of money."

"Then what? Surely not property," she laughed.

"The only property that I have come for is my father's sword and my mother's Bible. I understand that they have not been disposed of."

"Am I to believe that you violated my orders, entering my country with this handsome rogue, to risk your life for a sword and a book? You are a greater fool than your father."

Tavy grabbed hold of Rahzvon's taut arm to restrain him.

"Ahh...Mr. Sierzik, Kosdrevians have but one need for their father's sword—for the wedding ceremony. Have you returned to renew our relationship?" She stepped in front of him and looked smugly into his face. "I thought not. However, a wedding requires a bride."

Tavy tightened his grip on Rahzvon's arm.

"Your friend is wise," she observed Tavy's hand on Rahzvon's forearm. "The bride is a sensitive subject, is it not?" She walked away. "Do not fear, Mr. Rahzvon Sierzik, you shall see her one last time. She should be arriving within the hour with our mutual friend, the loyal Yagdub."

Rahzvon's face reddened. Tavy's blood boiled, but maintained his calm appearance, hoping to gain the trust of this wretched woman—no longer to carry out his aforementioned plan, but now to have the opportunity to escape and save the women.

Creazna moved in on Tavy and ran her fingers through his golden waves. "The three shall bring a decent price on the slave market. My curiosity is allowing you that last agonizing minute to look upon your intended bride's pitiful face. Which of the inferior young tarts have you chosen to be suitable for your life of peasantry?"

"Inferior?" Rahzvon glared at her. "One hair on her head is of greater value than you and your entire kingdom."

"Take him to the dungeon!" she snapped.

She stepped toward Tavy, who offered a welcoming smile.

"Bring this brown-eyed wonder to my quarters."

***

Guillaume entered the road to the castle. It was not long before he came upon Sven, bound and struggling. Guillaume dismounted and immediately recognized Allison's silk scarf, a gift that he had given to her months earlier. Seeing it secured, tight between Sven's teeth, Guillaume's adrenalin took over. He lunged at Sven and grabbed him by the shoulders.

"Where are they?" Guillaume shouted and rolled Sven over and untied the scarf. "Tell me now!"

"I shall tell you nothing," Sven grumbled.

Guillaume grabbed Sven's collar and pulled his head up to his, "Either you tell me or I shall drag you deep into the woods where only the wolves shall find you."

Sven looked to the forbidding forest on his left, "They are traveling in the carriage to the castle."

"Then what?" Guillaume shook him.

"They are to be taken to Devlin to be sold."

Guillaume dropped him in the dirt with disgust. Guillaume removed his handkerchief and gagged Sven. "Sorry, old man." He drug Sven down into the ditch and covered him with a few branches for safekeeping. He tied Allison's scarf about his neck, climbed on his horse and headed toward the castle.

Meanwhile, Rahzvon sat in the dungeon regretting his return and praying that Sophia's and the lives of his friends would be spared—even if it meant sacrificing his own. Tavy, on the other hand, strolled freely around the Princess' private quarters.

"Do you take a fancy to one of the female travelling companions?" Creazna asked suspiciously.

"They are, as ye say, but peasant lassies, m' lady."

"You prefer the upper class?"

"Aye...Miranda of Costellan is more to me likin'."

"Miranda? She is nauseating," the princess crinkled her nose.

"Aye, she hasna been blessed wi' yer great beauty, but she is one o' the wealthiest women in Spain."

"Do you not find beauty and wealth a more desirable pair, Mr. McTavish?"

"Aye, what man wouldna prefer it?" Trina's face flashed in his memory.

"Very well, remain here." *The ermine dress with the black diamonds!* she thought. She disappeared behind the door to the adjoining room.

Knowing that any number of scoundrels would be tempted to wait, he had urgent matters at hand. Tavy left by way of the balcony, scaled the wall to the courtyard below, and took refuge behind a large stack of barrels labeled gunpowder.

At the castle's drawbridge, the three women sat perfectly still in the carriage. The driver said something in gisaleon and then drove across the moat. Once inside the palace walls and beyond the guards posted at the entrance, the women made their move. They leapt from the carriage and scurried into the shadow of the wall, taking cover in the stable. Sophia peered out, checking what appeared to be the keep of the castle.

"Trina, stay here. Allison and I shall find a discreet means of entry. If we are caught, it shall be your task to escape and get word to our family."

Trina nodded anxiously and stepped back into the darkness, watching her friends steal across the courtyard and weaving in and out of secluded doorways. With only the company of the horses, Trina stood rigid, contemplating her possible escape.

A second later a large hand from behind, clamped over her mouth. Without hesitation, she shook her head, bit his hand and dug her nails into her captor's arm.

"Aghh!" he released her. Trina whirled around to see Tavy tending his fresh wounds.

"Henry!"

"Shh!"

"What are you—I am so very sorry—did I hurt you? I did not know—you know I would not—"

Trina's apologetic pleas ended when Tavy moved in, put his arms around her, and then gave her a silencing kiss.

"Extraordinary ...response, Mr. McTavish," she said, breathless.

"We need to be quiet," he whispered. "I ne'er wanted to see a lassie unharmed, more in me entire life."

"Oh," Trina melted, resting her head on his chest for a second. She flashed back to reality. "Henry, where are the others?"

"Rahzvon is in the dungeon and Zigmann—we left him guarding in the woods."

"In the dungeon? Oh, no, it is true. Before we attacked and bound him, Sven told us that Rahzvon would be captured," she reported with bitterness.

Tavy raised a brow at the courageous account.

"Sophia and Allison went to scout—to find a way into the castle. They left only minutes ago."

"I'll fetch 'em. I hae a plan to get Gypsy out o' there. That wretched woman will show him no mercy."

Shortly thereafter, the first part of his plan went into effect. Sophia boldly walked toward the guards posted outside of the throne room. The guards immediately arrested her and took her to the princess. Feeling considerably under-dressed for the occasion, Sophia stood before the beautifully clad princess.

"Which one are you?" Creazna asked impertinently.

"I am the future Mrs. Rahzvon Sierzik." Sophia held her head high.

"*You?*" Creazna laughed, looking at Sophia's boots.

"*I* did not have to ask him—Rahzvon proposed to me," Sophia said smugly.

"You may see the pathetic scoundrel. I shall take great pleasure in observing his response to your capture." She pointed at a guard. "Bring her to the dungeon. Has the sailor been found?"

"No, Your Highness."

Sophia sighed with relief.

"Useless idiots," she scowled.

Sophia followed without protest. Her heart ached when she saw Rahzvon sitting helplessly on the dirt floor of his cell.

"Rahzvon, your bride has come to bid you farewell," Creazna snickered.

Rahzvon got up and rushed to the barred door, only to see Sophia thrown into the adjacent cell. Creazna led her guards out, leaving Sophia and Rahzvon in dimly lit isolation.

"Phia , did they hurt you?"

"No, I was captured intently," she whispered.

"*Intentionally*, Phia?"

"I really cannot believe that you found that wretched Creazna attractive."

"*Phia*, I did not find her to be attractive— that is why I am here."

"Rahzvon, Tavy kissed Trina! Can you believe it?"

"What are you talking about?"

"Tavy found us and he kissed Trina and she bit his hand. Of course, he really did not deserve it and she is very sorry for the entire incident, the nail marks in his arms—not the kiss—she adored the kiss. Trina says that his kisses—"

"Hold it right there. We are in a dungeon about to be executed and you are discussing McTavish's kissing ability?"

"This is serious, for her! I was only trying to keep you abreast of the current situation. Calm down, Rahzvon. Tavy, is also an expert with explosives."

"Explosives?"

"Tavy is going to blow out that wall. Right over there," Sophia said pointing to the one behind him. "That is the reason I am here—to inform you of the plan of escape."

"An explosion?" Rahzvon's eyes widened.

"Rahzvon, you need not be so anxious. That wall will disappear very shortly and before you have chance to say 'thank you, Tavy,' we will be on our way back to Scotland to live happily ever after."

"Decimating that wall may free me, but what is his plan to get you out?"

Realizing the situation, Sophia looked at the cell door, panicked, and began screaming, "I will

never get out—I am doomed—we will never marry—
we will never travel to Italy!"

"Shh! Phia! McTavish surely knew that they
would put you in a separate cell. What did he say?"

"I do not know," she said fearfully tightening
her grip on the bars.

"Think, Phia, think."

"I cannot remember!"

"*Phia.*"

"I suppose that we shall have to wait and
pray."

"Remarkable insight, Little One."

Guillaume sat upon his horse at a crossroad,
considering to either, storm the castle alone and
demand the release of his companions, or to return
to the cottage and seek assistance to rescue them.
Time was running out and he knew that a wrong
decision could be life threatening for his friends. He
chose the latter and rode off toward Lillitheen's
home.

When Guillaume arrived, he was surprised to
find a black motorcar parked out front. He
dismounted and walked his horse discreetly to the
barn. *So they sent a backup force.* He crept beneath
the window with the view of the mountain, and
listened.

"We have our instructions, Madame. Please
bring the girls here, at once," a man commanded.

That will not happen in the near future,
Guillaume thought.

There was a moment of silence before
Lillitheen announced, "They are gone! Not a one is
here—woman or man."

"Gone! He is going to have our heads!" the
man remarked.

Guillaume shook his head, knowing that their fears were for naught as their leader, Sven, was a bit tied up for the present time. Knowing time was of the essence, Guillaume grew impatient. His need to get Lillithccn's advicc for rccruiting assistance was inhibited by these intruders. Guillaume listened while another question was proposed to Rahzvon's aunt.

"Madame, do you have any information regarding their departure?" the man asked gently.

The man's tone seemed to offer no immediate threat to Rahzvon's aunt, so Guillaume left promptly to return to the motorcar. *I will take the car into the village for help—that will stop them!*

Guillaume slithered around the long, black sedan to the driver's side and opened the door. He slid into the seat and closed the door as quietly as possible. He felt along the dashboard for the key. Nothing.

"No key?"

"No key, Zigmann."

Guillaume spun around. "Mr. McDonnally!"

"Is Sophia inside?" Hiram asked.

"No, no, sir. What are you doing here? Am I glad to see you! Sir, there is no time to waste!"

"Explain, *now*, Guillaume." Hiram leaned forward.

Guillaume explained the situation, from the visitors at the shack, to Sven's confession of the plan for the girls' fate. His suspicions that all were being held at the castle, led Hiram to lay on the horn. His associates arrived instantly.

"Take us to the Castle of Kosdrev and make haste!" Hiram instructed.

"Sir, I would like to apologize," Guillaume began.

"I think that it would be for the best if we refrain from any conversation," Hiram warned.

Guillaume nodded humbly.

The motorcar sped off down the narrow winding road. It was nearly midnight. When they arrived at the drawbridge, Guillaume held his breath, feeling certain that the car would be impounded and they would be imprisoned. Hiram motioned for the guard from his window. Hiram spoke in gisaleon. To Guillaume's astonishment, the car was given entry through the castle walls.

"Might I ask what you said to them, sir?" Guillaume inquired.

"No."

Suddenly, a large booming sound and a fiery blast at the base of the castle erupted as they crossed the moat.

Chapter X

"Savior"

"I ne'er was struck before that hour
With love so sudden and so sweet.
Her face it bloomed like a sweet flower
And stole my heart complete."

—John Clare

The car stopped abruptly. Hiram and Guillaume jumped out to the sight of Trina and Allison running toward them.

"Guillaume!" Allison called.

"Mr. McDonnally?" Trina caught her breath next to him.

Allison embraced Guillaume, admiring the scarf. "Sophia and Rahzvon are in the dungeon! Tavy blew up the wall to help them escape."

"Fools!" Hiram shouted. Several guards came into view, exiting the smoke-filled area, leading Rahzvon, Tavy and Sophia.

"Sophia!" Hiram called. He was about to run to her, when a half dozen guards approached. Hiram went peaceably, but whispered to Guillaume, Trina and Allison, "Say nothing."

Princess Creazna sat on her father's throne, screaming orders to her subjects in her native tongue when she caught a glimpse of the dashing Hiram. Her eyes widened in surprise of the stately gentleman before her. His appealing appearance led her from the throne to float in a dazed state toward the unexpected visitor.

"Man of every woman's dreams, identify yourself and your purpose for giving my eyes such uncommon pleasure." The princess walked around him, admiring the view.

Hiram remained stern and fixed in his position. "You have something that belongs to me and I have something of yours."

"Sounds intriguing, tall one."

"Release my niece and her friends."

"*Your* niece? Hmm...I do see the resemblance in the eyes and the hair. Pity she is not nearly as handsome. You do realize that she and her playmates have entered Kosdrev in defiance of my orders. Sierzik's failure to comply to my wishes is punishable by execution or life imprisonment—whichever I feel to be most beneficial."

"Does your king find your actions to be favorable?" Hiram asked with suspicion.

"My father is ill and decrepit. He is incapable of ruling Kosdrev," she shot back.

"Your talents as the ruler appear to be deficient, as well. Revolutions do not occur in kingdoms of just, omnipotent rulers."

"Silence! Your insolence does not become your handsome face. Do not underestimate me or you shall find yourself joining Rahzvon in his sentence."

"Likewise, you shan't underestimate me or you shall find yourself penniless and living amongst the rats of Devlin."

"How dare you! Arrest this man!"

The guards moved in, when Hiram spoke but two words, "McDonnally...Hiram."

The confident smile fled from Creazna's face.

"McDonnally of Scotland?" she choked out the words.

"Aye. You are familiar with the name? Might I refresh your failing memory? McDonnally—the clan who purchased your shipping fleet only yesterday—the fleet responsible for all export and import trade for Kosdrev."

"You are the man who purchased it from Alanvahs of Devlin?" she muttered.

"The very one. Aye, your betrothed is a very greedy man. He would sell his own mother and probably has done so. The fact is that the economy of Kosdrev is in my hands. Whether it thrives or shrivels and dies, is solely dependent on my desires. Now, enough of this; I want my niece, Rahzvon, and the sailor, brought here at once."

The guards looked to their furious princess for instruction.

In her hesitation, Hiram warned, "If any harm comes to any one of them—you shan't enjoy the consequences. I promise you that."

Creazna snarled at Hiram and then ordered, "Bring the prisoners." She stared at Hiram. The challenge was one that she could not resist.

"Mr. McDonnally, are you married?"

Hiram ignored her annoying inquiry.

"Your refusal to reply indicates that you are not married or that your wife is a miserable wretch. Both of which I find acceptable. Do you not find me to be beautiful, now that I have granted your desire to release my prisoners?"

Hiram glared at her. "Rahzvon's father, Gaelon, was one of my dearest friends. Be grateful that I have not chosen to avenge his death."

The side door opened and Sophia, Tavy, and Rahzvon were led to the throne. All three turned awestruck in seeing Hiram accompanying Guillaume, Allison and Trina.

"Uncle Hiram!" Sophia broke free and ran to him. They embraced while Hiram focused on Rahzvon. The young man read his thoughts and looked away to avoid his reprimanding eyes.

"Rahzvon, McTavish, we are leaving now." Hiram informed them. Rahzvon's face grew anxious.

"Did you procure that for which you came?" Hiram asked Rahzvon.

"No, sir."

"The princess and her subjects shall remain here. Go with him, McTavish. Make haste."

"Sir, it may take a few minutes," Rahzvon warned.

"Rahzvon, go. We shall wait."

Guillaume nudged Hiram. "Sir, there are two Kosdreven horses tied in the woods and the man who double-crossed Rahzvon is in the ditch, remember?" he whispered.

Hiram turned to Creazna, "Two of your horses are tied in the forest."

Hiram turned to Guillaume, "Which forest?"

Guillaume searched his brain, "Brandy Bog?"

Creazna rolled her eyes in disgust, "Rebandyn Tog!"

Guillaume shrugged and waited, but Hiram made no mention of Sven. Guillaume reluctantly nudged Hiram again. "Sir, the man."

Hiram leaned toward Guillaume. "It shan't hurt for him to remain there until morning. I shall send word later. We are actually doing him a favor—his hours are numbered as it is."

Guillaume gave a confirming nod.

Sophia and Rahzvon rode with Hiram in the motorcar to Lillitheen's cottage. Despite Rahzvon's error in judgment, Hiram felt that Rahzvon deserved the opportunity for a proper farewell to his aunt. Guillaume, Allison, Tavy and Trina followed in a carriage driven by a friend of Gaelon. Rahzvon sat with the metal chest on his lap and his father's sword at his feet. His success in procuring his inheritance was not as fulfilling as expected—having nearly lost Sophia and his dear friends. His strained relationship with Hiram was also discouraging. Rahzvon remained silent and glum. Next to Hiram, Sophia sat holding the bible, which had belonged to Rahzvon's mother. She looked up at her hero, never feeling more proud to be a member of the McDonnally clan. Sophia did not know the details of their release, and dared not ask her uncle until he was in better temperament. All that mattered was that she and her friends were returning safely home and Rahzvon was prepared to marry her—hopefully with her uncle's blessing.

In the carriage, Guillaume rode hand-in-hand with Allison. Their blue eyes locked in loving appreciation. Tavy, the confident lady's man, sat next to Trina. Several times, he turned over the token that she gave to him. He wanted to say something to convey his affection, but having never made a commitment to a woman, he was unsure of the procedure. He felt as though he would bust if he did not get it out and over with.

As they rode along, Trina watched out the window, seeing little of the night landscape. Instead, she reviewed her feelings for the unsophisticated sailor seated next to her. *He kissed me—despite my attack upon him. This is a good sign*, she thought, having believed that Tavy would never get over his feelings for Sophia. Out of the corner of her eye, she saw that he was turning her token. She felt that he had to be thinking of her, but questioned as to whether or not he would make it known. She waited patiently, knowing that she had all the time in the world, or at least until he shipped out again.

Tavy watched the two lovebirds, Guillaume and Allison, engaged in what appeared to be romantic whispers. He looked at Trina who remained focused on the window. His gaze lowered to her hand, then to the token, knowing that returning it, would initiate a conversation.

"Miss Dunmore?"

"*Trina*. Yes, Henry?" she turned with a hopeful smile.

"Trina, here, I'll be returnin' this to ya." He

placed the token in her hand. "It brought me good luck, I thank ya."

Trina stared at it in her palm. Had she been so wrong? She was crushed. She had imagined him carrying it with him forever, to remind him of her.

Tavy grinned, but then was disappointed to see her sudden look of distress. He realized that he had made a fatal mistake. To her surprise, he plucked the token from her hand and sat straight in the seat.

"If ye wouldna mind, I should like to keep this."

"No, I would not mind. In fact I had hoped that you would—keep it."

Tavy slid the token back into his pocket, reached over and took Trina's hand, and faced forward. Trina smiled with relief. Tavy grinned as if he had just made the greatest catch of the day.

The cruise from the Norwegian peninsula to Scotland was to be anything but pleasant for Rahzvon and friends. Each had knowingly acted irresponsibly. Hiram's conversation with the young people was never to be forgotten. It took place in Hiram's cabin on the second night of the cruise. Until then, Hiram had refused to speak to any of them, including his niece. Once they assembled in his cabin, as requested, Hiram stood silent before them, remembering Livia's last words: "Be grateful that they are safe and do not destroy the ship or I may not see you again, which I could not bear." His audience waited respectfully for him to speak. He folded his hands and stared at the floor.

"I am doing my blasted best to contain my anger, but I cannot imagine how six adults, young that you are, could be so foolish, so incredibly ignorant, and utterly irrational." He raised his head. "I can understand that your loyalty to Rahzvon instigated this stupidity, but there are limits within which normal, sane people abide."

Hiram looked to Rahzvon, "I do not have to tell you that I am appalled that you chose to continue this mission with these...these young women. That was precarious and unconscionable."

"Yes, sir," Rahzvon answered with his head held high.

"McTavish, you have a wealth of experience with danger and yet you were driven by your ego to become the hero. Blasting the dungeon wall? Did you actually believe that was a safe means of escape?"

"Not now, sir," Tavy replied, glancing toward Trina.

"Guillaume Zigmann." Guillaume stood and Hiram placed his hands on his shoulders. Guillaume lowered his head in shame.

Hiram began, "You, sir, are responsible for my success in locating your foolish friends. Without your assistance, the rest of you may have been greeting Creazna's executioner."

Guillaume raised his head, not believing his ears.

"Good work, Zigmann." He gave his shoulders a firm pat. Guillaume stood tall, grinning at Allison, but noted Rahzvon and Tavy's skeptical expressions.

Hiram then turned to the women.

"Miss Dunmore, we are not well-acquainted, but I highly recommend that in the future you choose your friends wisely and do not be swayed by their immature notions for adventure."

Hiram turned slowly to Allison. This was an awkward moment for him; having been a close companion in the past and the source of her heartbreak, he hesitated.

"I...I am glad that you are returning safely to your mother. Naomi has been beside herself with worry."

Allison nodded.

He turned to Sophia, who was busy admiring Rahzvon. "Excuse me, Sophia. I would like to speak with you privately. The rest of you may return to your quarters."

After they filed out of the cabin, Sophia spoke first. "Well, Uncle Hiram, it has been quite the little holiday, has it not?" she said with a bit of whimsy in her tone.

Hiram loomed above her, "Sophia McDonnally, I shall be leading this conversation."

"Yes, sir. I only think that you should know that—"

"Sophia!"

She lowered her head. Hiram lifted it with his finger beneath her chin.

"Sophia McDonnally, you have vexed me, deceived me, brought unnecessary grief to your entire family, forced me into an undesirable business arrangement—"

"You have purchased Kosdrev?" Sophia said ecstatically.

"Nay. *As I was saying*, you made me abandon my guest, as well as made a fool of me."

"Guest? What guest?"

"That is not the topic of this discussion."

"It is a woman, is it not? I can tell by the way in which you said 'guest'," she grinned with excitement.

Hiram sat down. "Sophia, I am tired. We are not discussing my social life."

Sophia immediately scooted next to him, "Social life? Uncle Hiram, you have to tell me—who is this woman?"

"I am not talking about her."

"It is a woman! Who is she? Please tell me, I shan't rest until I know."

"Absolutely not, Sophia."

"You met her in London—at the conference!"

"No—well, yes."

"A business woman!"

"No, Sophia, Livy has nothing to do with business."

"Livy? *Livy*?...Livia Nichols? The author of *If Only We Had Kissed*!"

Hiram rolled his eyes in defeat and dropped back on the bed.

"Uncle, how did you find her? It was Naomi—she sent her to the conference. I knew she would find—"

Hiram sat up, "Stop, stop, stop, Sophia! It was not Naomi. We found each other by accident."

"*Accident*? Uncle Hiram it was God's will. You love her and she loves you. How romantic," she said dreamily. "Uncle Hiram, I have to ask you, is it true?"

"What *now*, Sophia?" he asked, exhausted by her ranting.

"Did you really...*not* kiss her?"

Hiram shot up from the bed. "My private life is not *your* business, Miss McDonnally!" He began to pace, restricted as it was in the cabin.

"Begging your pardon, but a published book could hardly be considered private, Uncle Hiram."

"I asked you to remain here, so that we could discuss *your* behavior—not mine."

"Very, well, I apologize, Uncle. I am listening...How *did* I make a fool of you?"

"Dare the alleged Parisian tourist ask?"

"I did not want you to worry," she smiled and shrugged one shoulder.

"How did you expect me to react when your mother arrived, discrediting your alibi of the trip to France?"

"I admit, a slight oversight on my part. Next time, I shall be more careful," Sophia said, swinging her ugly boots on the side of the bed.

"As long as you are living under my roof there shan't be a next time."

"Yes, sir," she let out an indifferent sigh, believing she would soon be married to Rahzvon.

"Sophia, why do you vex me so? Can you not regard me with a little more respect and consideration?" Hiram said wearily.

"That is not true. I love and respect you. As for vexation, I am certain that you have learned there is not a woman on this earth that would not vex you in one way or another. It is your misperception. As women, we have great difficulty trying to make men understand how we think. Instead of listening to us, you simply consider us to be a vexation and go about your business. The problem is not with me, or Livia, or Naomi, or anyone else—it is with you...and all men."

Hiram raised a brow to her bold remark.

"Now, Uncle, I bid you goodnight for I really need to discuss my wedding plans with Rahzvon."

"Wedding?" Hiram's voice rose.

"Propose to Livia and we can make it a double ceremony. I shan't mind. See you at breakfast!" she smiled and slipped out of the door.

Rahzvon sat on the bed in his cabin. He had finished calculating the sum of his inheritance, which was greater than he had expected. Despite this discovery, he felt a deep sadness; he could not thank his late father for the wonderful gift. Rahzvon's relationship with Gaelon was amiable, but typically, like any father and son, they nearly came to blows on a few occasions. Rahzvon's mother had passed on when he was a boy and his only sibling, Gaelon the II, had left Kosdrev at the age of twenty-one when Rahzvon was nine years old. His brother had only returned once to see his family, the year prior to their father's death.

Gaelon II, not unlike his father, was a financial wizard. He became independently wealthy before his thirtieth birthday. Both, Rahzvon's wish for his brother to receive word in time to prevent their father's execution, and his desire for his brother to rescue him from his homeless state afterwards, had failed to come true. His brother's negligence left Rahzvon bitter and resentful.

Rahzvon sat the chest on the floor, leaned back in the berth, and analyzed the man he had become—a man of significant means without a country or family, yet drawn into the McDonnally clan. He had significant financial security to create a future for Sophia, without relying on her inheritance, but not a hint as to a plan for the upcoming years.

Chapter XI

"In A Stew"

"Variety's the very spice of life
That gives it all its flavour."

—William Cowper

Rahzvon had promised Sophia, love and a life with him—*but what life?* he thought. Where and doing what? He knew that one could never accuse him of being lazy. Once motivated, he worked to near obsession. Now he lay there dumbfounded, with no motivation, no path to follow. He had no knowledge of business, no interest in farming, although he loved horses. He had no desire to continue his education. The myriad of possible occupations was overwhelming, but in his mind, uninspiring.

He looked over the edge of the bed to the box, below. Its contents had an incredible power over his once simple life. For a split second, the idea of tossing it overboard was almost worthy of consideration. He had his fortune, but with it, came expectations—Sophia's. No fault of hers, he realized, aware that he was the one who had spoken of marriage in conjunction with procurement of his fortune.

He sat up, "Yes, I love her." He imagined being her husband, but not at all prepared for the future after their wedding day. He dropped to his pillow and closed his eyes. Sophia's knock disturbed that one moment of peace.

"Rahzvon, may I come in?"

"Yes, Phia, for a minute."

When she entered, Rahzvon got up and offered her the only available chair.

Sophia sat beaming with excitement. "Do you want to get married in the church or in my uncle's garden?"

"Phia, have you forgotten? I have not asked you, as yet."

Sophia stood up, "Yes, you did."

Rahzvon sat down on the bed. "No, I did not." A picture of pure frustration, he ran his fingers through his hair, rubbing his scalp. He let out a sigh and looked up at her. "I do not deny that we spoke of marrying on several occasions, but I have *not* formally proposed."

"Well then, go ahead. I am ready," she said with her impish smile.

He stood up, "*I* am not ready, Phia. This will be on my terms. The time and place will be my choice."

Sophia reached up and ran her hand over the stubble of his beard. "The deck is glorious right now. The stars look like little beacons calling to us to join them," she said softly.

"No, Phia." He looked away.

"Being on a ship," she traced a little heart on his cheek with her finger, "the captain could marry us tonight."

Rahzvon took her wrists and pulled her hands away from his face. "You are incorrigible, Little One. No more of this. You need to get out of my cabin and back to yours. If your uncle finds you here, I will be swimming to Scotland under those little beacons."

"What about my goodnight kiss?"

"Not in here. Come along, I will walk you back to your cabin."

"I cannot believe Uncle Hiram assigned me the cabin on the other end of the ship, next to his," she pouted as they left.

"I can. Think of it this way—we can take long walks together between them."

"I would rather be at home, walking down the aisle of the church together," she muttered.

Rahzvon glanced down at his anxious future bride-to-be and offered her his arm.

"Phia?"

"Yes," she replied with new hope.

"What occupation do you imagine for me?"

"Occupation? Hmm? I never thought about it. Do you have to have one?"

"Of course I do." Annoyed, he inquired, "You do not expect me to make repairs with Albert or remain a stable boy for the rest of my life, do you?"

"Rahzvon, why are you so angry?"

"I am *not*." He stepped away. "I should not have mentioned it."

Sophia said nothing. He took her hand and they continued until they reached the cabin.

"Good night," he said abruptly.

"I shall be happy—no matter what line of work you choose. Good night," she said solemnly and opened the door.

"*Phia?*"

She stopped without turning.

"I *am* sorry. Forgive me," he said sincerely.

She turned and looked up with concern. "Rahzvon, am I to become Mrs. Sierzik?"

"Why would you ask, when you know that our future was the basis for my trip to Kosdrev?"

"You have had your inheritance but a few days and you have already become a different man—one with whom I am not familiar."

"Money changes people. It forces one to make decisions," he said bluntly. "I am not certain that I am prepared for...for any of it." He walked away to the deck railing.

Sophia gave him a second look, then entered her cabin and closed the door.

Rahzvon stared out across the sea remembering how the first voyage began with Sophia unexpectedly arriving next to him. He had been so glad to see her and now he had walked away leaving her, as though she were responsible for his fears and apprehension.

"Son, what is troubling you?" Hiram asked approaching him from behind.

"*Mr. McDonnally?*" Rahzvon turned back to the sea. "Everything, sir."

"I am listening. No doubt, my niece is involved."

"Sir, I am ashamed to admit this to you, of all people, but I am confused—aimless."

"That is not uncommon for a man who has lost his country."

"The money, Sophia, my life...it should all fit together like a puzzle, but it does not."

"It rarely does, Rahzvon."

Rahzvon turned to face Hiram. "Sir, I do not know where to begin. You are aware that I want to marry your niece, but I have never had money, a wife, and a home."

"I have had but two of the three and I still do not have the answers."

"I am at a loss as to what profession to enter. My experience is limited."

"You need not decide tonight. Mark my words: unwarranted worry and unsupervised anger breeds disaster for tomorrow. I am not a very religious man, but I have learned to give the Almighty the opportunity to provide the solutions. Trust me, considering that it took an act of God for you to procure your inheritance." He raised a brow. "Good night, Mr. Sierzik."

"Good night, sir."

In Lochmoor Glen, the parents of the returning adventurers shared a mutual frame of mind. It was akin to that of parents whose children who had been found playing with matches—relief and gratitude for their safety, combined with anger and disappointment for their progenies' foolishness. The Dugans, Tavy's adoptive parents, on holiday with relatives in the Highlands, were spared the exasperation of Tavy's misadventure. It would be several weeks before the incident in Kosdrev would lay to rest.

In the meantime, Hiram picked up where he left off, in the renewed relationship with Livia Nichols, now visiting his home. Livia began plans for her future childcare facility and Edward and Naomi were enjoying their role as surrogate parents to the Wheaton children.

The younger generation was equally involved in time-consuming activities after their return. Sophia, naturally, was privately preparing for her wedding, despite Rahzvon's withdrawn behavior. He was investigating possibilities for employment, while Guillaume was busy with application forms for architectural firms, which Allison reviewed for location and stability. Trina Dunmore sought excuses to extend her stay in Lochmoor Glen in order to reside near Henry McTavish, who conveniently 'missed the boat' which set sail for three months of sea duty.

Despite the mixed feelings over the journey to Kosdrev, Naomi planned an outing of *reunion* at Duncan Ridge with the straying offspring, rather than a *welcome home* celebration. Meetings for the arrangements were scheduled at Brachney Hall. Naomi met with the women in the parlor to organize the foodstuffs, while Edward and the men organized the sporting events in the library. Hannah remained at McDonnally Manor. Having spent most of her life in the café, she chose to remain uninvolved with any decisions pertaining to food.

Naomi began the discussion, "I thought that we would have haggis for the entre."

"Not again, we always have haggis," Sophia complained.

"Then pheasant," Naomi offered.

Her daughter, Allison, cut in, "Guillaume does not like pheasant. I think ham would be better."

Beatrice shook her head, "No, three of the Wheaton girls refuse to eat pork of any kind, since they witnessed their father slaughtering their pig, McCoy."

"We will have to have beef," Sophia deduced.

"*Beef*? I have been cooking with beef for the last week, because the venison that I ordered was sent to the wrong household," Eloise reminded. "But if that is what you want…"

"We could have cod," Trina suggested, in her preoccupation with the amorous sailor.

"Yes, an excellent idea, I have not had a good fish dinner in months," Beatrice added.

"No, no," Naomi disagreed, "I worry about bones with the children."

"Mother, the girls have been raised on fish. Bruce would take them fishing every other weekend," Allison contradicted.

Naomi left her chair, "All the same, I do not want to spend the meal inspecting for bones for them. I am not comfortable relying on the cook and her…questionable eyesight. Any suggestions, Livia?"

Livia shook her head.

Naomi thought for a moment, and then remembered her first cooking adventure with Edward. "Stew! Why not a nice vegetable stew with very little meat?"

"As long as there is no pheasant in it," Allison warned.

"All agreed?" Naomi asked.

Everyone nodded skeptically.

"Very well. I shall inform Edward that he is in charge of the stew. He takes great pride in his recipe. That takes care of the entrée. We can accompany it with breads and fruit. Any suggestion for afters?" Naomi polled the group.

"Rahzvon adores apple tarts," Sophia spoke up.

"That is not a good idea, Sophia. Guillaume refuses to eat tarts. He ate too many at the festival in Glasgow." Allison chuckled a little, "Even smelling them makes him queasy."

Sophia stopped rocking and stood up, "Allison, we cannot plan this entire outing around Guillaume's stomach!"

Allison left the divan and challenged Sophia, face-to-face. "It is not my fault that he is sensitive, Sophia! Guillaume's preferences are important—he is family!"

"I am marrying Rahzvon and he will become a McDonnally!" Sophia blurted out without thinking.

Naomi quickly intervened, "Ladies, ladies! We are planning a pleasant outing, not preparing for war. Any ideas, Livia?"

Livia shrugged.

Naomi smiled. "Well...I could order some Italian ice cream from Mrs. Pellegrini."

Allison shook her head, "No, goes right through Guillaume."

Sophia glared at Allison.

Naomi gave Sophia a warning look.

"Everyone likes carrot cake, and...it is Edward's favorite. Would that be amenable to everyone?"

"As long as it has a drizzle over it," Sophia muttered.

Allison tightened her lips and shook her head. "Too much drizzle irritates Guillaume. It is *so* messy."

Sophia's dark eyes objected.

Naomi quickly cut in, "That is not a problem. We will serve the drizzle on the side, so that everyone can...*drizzle* as much or little as they desire." Naomi sighed. "Now for the beverages. Livia, any suggestions?" Naomi asked politely, again trying to make her guest feel involved.

Livia shook her head.

"A cool lemon drink," Sophia spoke up.

Allison gave a quick headshake, "Too much acid—Guillaume would be ill all day."

Trina knitted her brows, having no idea that her former beau's constitution was so fragile.

"Guillaume can have water! I want lemon drink!" Sophia shouted.

"Sophia, please lower your voice," Naomi insisted.

"Everyone may have the beverage of their choice," Naomi resolved, preferring not to venture further into the possibilities. "Please give your requests to the cook. Can you think of anything else, Livia?"

Livia shook her head, declining with only one desire—to remain neutral in the *menu madness*.

In the library, Edward stood at the end of the table leading the discussion of the activities for the outing. After overhearing the occasional outbursts from the dining room, he commented, "Too many hens, not enough chickens." The men chuckled and then looked curiously at one another."

"Is that the saying?" Guillaume asked.

Edward ignored him and began, "Now, I am open for suggestions?"

"We could have a horse race," Guillaume suggested.

"Nay," Hiram shook his head. "The women shan't care to participate."

"They need not. They can cheer us on," Guillaume said, anxious to show off his skills in horsemanship.

Suspicious, Rahzvon ran his hand down the side of his face, "Zigmann, how are we to determine which horse each man rides?"

"Does it matter? I will take Duff."

With a little laugh, Rahzvon dropped back in his chair. "Ah... no. Duff can outrun any horse in a thirty-mile radius of the village. Is that not what you said Mr. McDonnally?" Rahzvon turned to Hiram.

"Aye, 'tis true."

Guillaume stood up, flipping back his chair. "Are you accusing me of choosing Duff to seek an advantage?" Guillaume retorted. "A good horseman can win, no matter what the mount!"

Rahzvon gave a wave of disbelief. "You are daft, Zigmann. If you believe that—ride the Dugan mule," Rahzvon snickered.

"I would, but they took Jock with them!"

"Enough, gentlemen." Edward demanded. "The horse race is out."

Amused by the sparring, Hiram grinned, resting his elbow on the table and his chin on his fist.

Guillaume scowled and sat down. His face brightened. "Forget the horses; we can have a dog race."

Rahzvon rolled his eyes upward. "Zigmann, Heidi and Rusty are the only two dogs and your dog can outrun Heidi by a mile."

"Only because Sophie feeds Heidi every chance she gets," Guillaume said under his breath.

Rahzvon went up and over the table after him.

Hiram grabbed Rahzvon's arm and pulled him back to his chair. "Easy, lad. Cricket anyone?" Hiram quickly suggested.

"Hiram, you know that I cannot play, since my injuries," Edward objected.

"*Edward,* you are making excuses for your pathetic athletic abilities." Hiram casually leaned back in his chair and folded his hands behind his head.

Edward approached Hiram's side of the table, "I am not! I have not had adequate time in which to heal."

Hiram looked away, tight-lipped and struggling to withhold his laughter with his pronounced telltale dimples.

"You only suggested cricket because you were the champion and you want to show off for Miss Nichols," Edward declared.

Hiram's head jerked toward Edward and left his chair. "That is not true! I do not need to display my superior cricket playing to impress Livia. She is quite content with my other talents."

Rahzvon looked to Hiram and raised a brow. Hiram quickly qualified his statement. "*My* business savvy, and...my singing—blast it!" He slammed his fist to the table and walked over to the bookshelves.

Edward glared at Hiram, shook his head, and then announced, "The games are out, too. Are there any other suggestions?"

The room was silent.

Finally, Rahzvon spoke, "We could make kites and have a flying contest. The children would enjoy it."

Hiram looked toward the group with disapproval.

"Excellent idea, Rahzvon," Edward commended.

"Highest altitude, longest duration in the air?" Guillaume squinted at Rahzvon.

"You are on, Zigmann." Rahzvon offered him a handshake.

Guillaume shook it. "Teams? May the best man and woman win."

Hiram, having poor experience with kite construction and fearing embarrassment in Livia's presence, moved back to the table.

"Nay. Sorry Rahzvon, but that is a poor suggestion."

"How so, Hiram?" Edward inquired suspiciously.

"It...it is dangerous."

"Dangerous?" Guillaume looked puzzled, as did the others.

"For the children. We have to consider the children," Hiram fumbled. "The string may cut their wee hands and they may become entangled."

His audience listened with acute skepticism.

"Right, Hiram, and the string could get caught around their necks and they could be dangling from the trees," Edward mocked. "A bit overprotective, eh, Hiram? And I am not referring to the children."

Hiram moved into his face. "What are you insinuating, Edward?"

"Only that I happen to know that the one and only kite that you ever produced had enough wood in it to prevent a twister from lifting it off the ground."

"It may not have left the ground, but at least it was not *I* who was stuck up in a tree for an hour trying to retrieve it, nor did I require two men and a ladder to get *me* down!"

Rahzvon and Guillaume remained silent.

"It is settled, three to one in favor of the kites," Edward announced.

"We never voted!" Hiram pounded his fist on the table.

"Very well, a recount is desired. All in favor of the kite activity, say *aye*—aye!"

Rahzvon and Guillaume looked toward each other in solidarity once again. Dare they vote against Hiram. His threatening stare was upon them. Rahzvon did not want to fall any further from Hiram's good graces and Guillaume had enjoyed Hiram's support for the first time when he complimented him while on the ship. However, their competitive spirit overrode their fear of angering Hiram.

"Aye!" they replied in unison.

"Opposed?" Edward asked.

Hiram's ebony eyes shot daggers toward his opponents, before he left the library.

"All rise," Edward said, "the meeting is adjourned."

That evening Naomi and Edward compared notes on the preparations for the reunion.

"Dearest, how did the meeting fair?" Naomi asked Edward while braiding Corinne's hair.

"Everyone was present," Edward said behind a copy of *The Lost World*, a novel satisfying his new craving for science fiction.

"What activities did you select? Croquet or cricket?"

Edward paused, "Have you been speaking with Hiram?" he squinted with suspicion.

"No, love, why do you ask?"

"We are not playing either one. Some members of the group voted against it," he mumbled, covering for *his* disapproval of the two activities.

"Which members?"

"Naomi, must you know every detail of the meeting? You should have hosted it yourself," he said annoyed.

"Corinne, Mr. McDonnally did not mean to snap at me. He is in ill-temper for some unknown reason," Naomi said trying to hide her displeasure.

Corinne nodded trying not to pull her hair from Naomi's hands.

"I beg your pardon. May I ask what activities were chosen or is that a secret, Edward?"

"We are having a kite competition."

"Kites, mum, I must tell Marvel—she loves kites!" Corinne slipped away as Naomi finished tying the last ribbon.

"What else?" Naomi asked placing the brush and comb in the metal tin.

"Nothing else." Edward said behind the book.

"Only kite flying? What if there is no wind?"

Edward lowered the book and stared blankly. "*They* never considered that possibility."

"*Men.* I suggest that you come up with an alternative, as well. You can call them together again."

"I shan't," he said indignantly.

"Why?"

"They do not work well together as a group."

Naomi grinned. "We did note a bit of dissonance in the library. I can empathize with you. We had a few problems in compromising, as well. Incidentally, you will be preparing the stew," she patted his shoulder.

"Stew? No, no—the cook can do that. I am not having everyone make sport of my culinary creations. Absolutely not."

"Edward, it is has been decided and cannot be overruled. You should be happy, I convinced them to have carrot cake for afters."

"*Naomi,*" he whined. Who is hosting this event?" he sarcastically.

"I am." She kissed his forehead, "It will be delicious, and romantically sentimental." She paced a few steps and then sat down next to him.

"Edward?"

"What is it now, Naomi? I detect that familiar apprehension in your voice."

"We have a small problem...about the outing."

"Another one?" he asked wearily.

"We have an unexpected guest coming, dear," she said hesitantly.

Edward turned and dropped the book. He took Naomi by the shoulders, "Naomi! The baby! You are with child?"

"No, no, Edward, is that *all* you think about? No, another guest is coming."

"Daniel? Ah, that is a problem; he shan't have a kite prepared."

"Yes, Daniel is coming, but I am referring to someone who is coming at Hannah's invitation."

"Hannah is family. I am certain that we will approve of anyone she chooses to be her escort."

"Even if it is Zedidiah Hartstrum?" Naomi cringed, waiting for his response.

Chapter XII

"Passing the Buck"

"Women are like teabags.
We don't know our true strength
Until we are in hot water!"

—Eleanor Roosevelt

Edward stood up. His eyes bugged out just before deep creases appeared above the bridge of his nose. "Naomi, tell me that you did not just say that snake, Hartstrum?"

"I did, love."

"Too many hours over that hot stove in the café—my niece has cooked her brain. We need to get the woman a physician."

"Edward, that is an awful thing to say. Now, you cannot deny that Zed is eyed by every unattached woman in the village."

"*Zed?* They are all daft! Naomi, you were there—Hannah was there. He did his best to humiliate Hiram—her *twin* brother. She heard what he said, that arrogant jack—"

"Edward, shh! The children!"

"Naomi, if he arrives with Hannah, those children will be witnessing a great deal more than one slightly strong word. The outing will make the school meeting seem like a Sunday service in comparison. After Hiram disassembles *Zed*, he will disown his sister. Hiram walks around like a boiler. It is only a matter of time, Naomi. All that anger is churning inside of him. I witnessed the preview at the meeting only a few hours ago." Edward stood over her, "You are going to tell him, Naomi. Hiram has to be warned in advance."

"I am not. I paid my dues up at Hailes Crag. *You* can tell him."

"Not I. He is angry with me about the contest. You must, Naomi; it is your duty as hostess to this event."

"No, Edward."

"Naomi, No one is in the mood to witness another battle of Hiram versus Hartstrum."

"He is *your* nephew; you notify him."

"*Our* nephew. Naomi, I am still recovering from my accident. Do you want to be responsible for my relapse?"

"Edward, I refuse."

"Very well, I shall find someone else, *who cares.*" He contemplated the possible candidates. He considered Sophia; she had a knack for making light of everything. Then, Eloise; Hiram would never go berserk with her, for fear she would fall to tears or faint. He pondered a while longer and came to the conclusion, "Livia!"

"Edward Caleb McDonnally, you would not dare!"

"Livia is perfect for the task; she has a calming effect on Hiram. We owe Hiram this consideration, Naomi."

"Edward you cannot involve Livia," Naomi said adamantly. "Hiram does not approve of interference in his private life."

"I can and I shall, if it will prevent my home from becoming a crime scene. Naomi, my new tool shed is at risk!"

Naomi threw her hands up and went to the other side of the room. "I wash my hands of the entire ordeal; I shall have no part in it."

"You need not be involved. All you need do, is invite Livia to tea—I shall handle it from there."

"Absolutely not."

"Naomi, how would it appear if *I* were to invite Livia? Once Hiram discovered it, there would be no outing—you would be hosting my funeral service!"

Naomi rolled her eyes, biting her bottom lip to control her anger.

"A simple invitation, Naomi. Nothing more, nothing less."

Naomi took an exasperated breath and left the room in a huff.

At four o'clock, Livia sat with Naomi and Edward in the drawing room of Brachney Hall.

After offering the refreshments, Edward began his strategy, "Naomi and I—"

"*Edward*, Livia, you shall have to excuse me, I need to speak to the cook about the menu."

"*Naomi*, I really think that—" he felt Naomi's shoe give his an effective nudge.

"Very well," he agreed. While Naomi rushed to the kitchen, Edward presented the awkward and potentially dangerous situation of Zed's invitation.

"Livia, do you recall the guest speaker at the school meeting."

"I shan't soon forget him. That man is one person who I do not care to cross paths with in the near future." Livia sipped her tea.

Edward half-smiled, "I am sorry to inform you, but you shall. Hannah has invited him to the outing."

Livia dropped her teacup, but his quick hands recovered it. Livia tried to fathom the repercussions.

"He is going to be at the outing...with *my* Hi—Hiram?"

"Yes, Livia. I regret that it is true."

"This is a frightful situation."

"I know...that is why we asked you here tonight. We have seen the change in Hiram, since you arrived. We, Naomi and I, felt that you were the one person who was capable of, shall we say, gently breaking the news to him."

"Me?" Livia left her chair and started pacing. "No, no, I could not. You do not understand—he has a terrible temper."

"Oh, I *understand*. Livia, you could surely notify him in such a way, so as not to upset him. It is only for one short day."

Livia stopped and looked helplessly around the room, caught in Edward's snare without a means of escape.

"Please, Livia. You would not want the outing to be a disaster?" he warned.

Livia thought for a minute in dread of the encounter. She debated which would be the lesser of the two evils—watching Hiram explode at the reunion, or telling him in advance.

To Edward's surprise, Hiram arrived a half hour later to fetch Livia.

"What *was* the actual purpose of this invitation, Edward?" Hiram asked as he stepped into the drawing room.

Edward quickly hustled Hiram off to the library. "Naomi probably wanted to speak privately with Livia," he whispered in the hall.

"About?"

"Women things, I suppose."

"Is Naomi well?" Hiram asked with concern.

"She is...do you have the design for your kite, old man?" Edward grinned as they entered the room.

"I shall. Do not concern yourself." Hiram looked to the window, then to Edward. "I have been thinking. Daniel shall be arriving tomorrow afternoon to accompany Beatrice, leaving Hannah to be the only woman without an escort. I am considering inviting George Hicks."

"Your accountant! Are you mad?"

"Nay, he is a well-groomed, intelligent chap."

"*Hiram*, the man has never smiled in his life."

"Perhaps he needs cheering up."

"He is dull, boring—silent."

"Hannah is relatively withdrawn, as well."

"Your sister owned a café. She is not *withdrawn*; she is very outgoing, and would be bored stiff with that stuffed shirt. That is a simply terrible idea."

"Do you have a better one, someone more outspoken?

"I know of someone. Better? Definitely not." Edward closed his eyes.

The day prior to the outing, Hannah took advantage of the glorious weather and strolled along the drive of her brother's home, admiring the blooming heather. She turned to an arriving carriage, out of which a gentleman of nearly her age, stepped out. She noted his familiar facial structure. He smiled at her.

"Good morning, Madame," he bowed his head.

Rahzvon, he looks like Rahzvon. "Good morning, sir," she said hesitantly.

"Lovely day," he offered.

"Yes, very pleasant."

"I have come to see my brother."

"Rahzvon—you are his brother," she said confidently.

He stepped closer. "Yes, yes I am. May I introduce myself—Gaelon Sierzik II."

"I am Hannah. This is my brother Hiram's estate." She motioned toward the mansion. "Please come in. Rahzvon is inside with my daughter."

"Thank you."

Gaelon followed Hannah inside. He was admiring the mammoth hallway, when Hannah motioned.

"In here," she pointed toward the parlor.

Gaelon had no sooner entered the archway, when Sophia exclaimed, "I cannot believe my eyes! Rahzvon, he looks like you!"

Gaelon chuckled and Rahzvon guardedly left his chair at the sight of his estranged sibling.

"Gaelon," Rahzvon said lacking any emotion.

Gaelon? Sophia thought.

"*Bortigreg myn rertes*, Rahzvon."

"May I present Sophia McDonnally," Rahzvon said, without so much as a smile.

"My pleasure, Miss McDonnally. You should be extremely proud to share your uncle's name. Hiram has quite an impressive reputation." He kissed her hand.

"Thank you, yes I am, sir," she said shyly removing her hand from his.

Rahzvon cautiously viewed the scene.

"I, too, see the lovely resemblance." He turned toward Hannah.

"My mother, Hannah," Sophia grinned.

"Yes, I have had the honor."

Sophia raised a questioning brow and turned to Rahzvon.

"My older brother, Gaelon II."

Brother? Sophia looked peeved toward Rahzvon. "You never mentioned a brother," she whispered scornfully.

"Sophia," Hannah cut in, "I need to speak with you. Now."

Sophia threw Rahzvon a piercing glance and said, in passing to the hall, "Welcome to McDonnally Manor, Mr. Sierzik."

"Thank you," Gaelon waved to her. He turned to his brother who had sat down, seemingly annoyed with his presence.

"She is quite beautiful, Rahzvon."

"She is. Why are you here?" he asked with contempt.

Gaelon sat down across from him.

"Rahzvon, I was in Hong Kong when I got word about Father. I immediately returned to Kosdrev, but you were gone."

"*Banished*, Gaelon, *banished*. It was only by God's mercy that I was not executed, as well."

"I had no idea as to your destination."

"Nor did I," Rahzvon said sharply, leaving the chair.

"Belshum returned to Kosdrev and informed me of your recent return home and contacted me in India. I left the moment I heard. Rumor of Mr. McDonnally's intervention, brought me here."

"*Home?* It was never home to you. Now that you have found me, and you can see that I am in want of nothing, you may leave."

Gaelon walked over to him. "I never doubted that, Rahzvon. You have always been competently independent."

"How would you know? You left before my tenth birthday," Rahzvon refuted.

"I understand your anger with me, but I had hoped to become better acquainted. You are the only family that I have."

Rahzvon stared at his once idolized brother, debating whether he dare risk renewing the relationship.

"You have become quite a man, little brother."

"What did you expect from one who spends his days at physical labor?" Rahzvon mocked.

"I never expected that we would look quite so similar as adults."

Rahzvon showed no sign of approval for this comment.

"I *did* try to find you, Rahzvon."

"So you say."

Hiram stepped into the parlor, "I beg your pardon."

Rahzvon and his brother turned.

"Mr. McDonnally, my brother Gaelon," he said, lacking enthusiasm.

Hiram shook Gaelon's hand. "I knew your father, Gaelon. He was a dear friend of mine. I had great respect for him."

"And I for you, sir. Your reputation is known the world over. I heard of your assistance to my brother, in Kosdrev. I thank you."

Rahzvon broke in, "You need not extend your gratitude on my behalf, I have already done so."

Hiram took a breath. "Gaelon, you are welcome to stay here for the duration of your visit."

"I appreciate your offer, but the length of my stay is undetermined," he looked uneasily at his brother.

Hiram observed Rahzvon's discontented expression. "Pleasure meeting you. I shall take leave of you. I have a previous engagement. I hope to see the two of you at tea."

"We would be honored, sir," Gaelon replied.

Meanwhile, Sophia pouted at the kitchen table, "I cannot believe that he did not tell me that he had a brother."

"Perhaps, he did not want you to know. He did not appear to be overjoyed with his arrival. Many were not aware that I had a brother," Hannah explained.

"Is it not amazing how similar they are? It is like a looking glass into the future. That is what Rahzvon will look like when he is old," Sophia said examining an apple from the bowl.

"Old? Gaelon is probably, my age," Hannah scoffed.

"He is quite a looker."

"*Sophia,* there is more to a man than his appearance?"

Sophia nodded, waited then grinned teasingly. "Mother, you have to admit that he is handsome."

"Well, of course, he looks just like Rahzvon."

"Mother! You *do* think Rahzvon is magnificent!"

"Sophia, many men are appealing to the eye, but character is of greater importance."

"Rahzvon is more honorable than you could possibly know. I could tell you things about him that would astonish you."

"Are you planning to share an example with me?"

"Yes. Rahzvon refused to *kiss* me in my nightgown," Sophia announced proudly.

"Sophia!

"Rahzvon thinks it inappropriate."

"What were you doing dressed like that in his presence?"

"Homeless in the woods," Sophia said nonchalantly.

"Explain, Miss McDonnally," Hannah demanded.

"Mother, you always imagine the worst. I was locked out of the house. It was all very innocent, although it was very difficult convincing Uncle Hiram of that at two in the morning. He nearly killed

Rahzvon. Thanks to me, Gaelon still has a brother to visit."

"Phia," Rahzvon appeared in the doorway.

"Yes?"

"Could you please have Eloise direct Gaelon to his room?"

Sophia gave a little grin to her mother, "Yes, I shall tell her. She is in the garden."

Rahzvon glanced at Hannah, and then made a double take of her glare.

As Sophia passed Gaelon she looked up, "I hope that you shall enjoy your stay. My mother is visiting...*alone*, as well." Sophia continued to the garden to find Eloise.

Rahzvon rolled his eyes.

Gaelon looked toward the very embarrassed mother who was rearranging the apples in the bowl, when Eloise entered the backdoor and wiped her hands on her apron.

"Welcome, sir. Follow me. You will be in the north wing."

Gaelon followed and Rahzvon walked out into the garden where Sophia was gathering a bouquet.

"What are you doing?" he asked.

"Being creative. Mother can deliver these to Gaelon's room."

"Phia, do not play matchmaker with my brother," he reprimanded.

"Why not? He seems to be charming, like yourself. Do I detect some fratertal animosity toward your brother?"

Despite his anger with Gaelon, Rahzvon burst out laughing. "*Fratertal?* What is that—a cross between a frog and a turtle?" he teased.

"At least you are smiling, now. My intuition is correct; you do not like your brother very much, do you not?"

Rahzvon took a breath. "I am indifferent. I barely know the man and not quite sure if I care to."

"I think that you should take the time to learn more about him. He *is* your only sibling. Or are there more?" she added sarcastically.

Rahzvon shook his head.

"I need to become better acquainted, as well. I have no brothers or sisters. He shall be my brother-in-law. A brother—how nice." She stepped on the back stoop and turned to Rahzvon. Her eyes grew large. "Oh dear, if he marries mother, he shall be my brother-in-law and my stepfather!"

Rahzvon stopped and thought about it. *She actually said something that made sense.* "Assuming that I propose," he teased.

Sophia ignored his remark, carried the flowers into the kitchen, and placed them in water in a vase that she found on the bottom pantry shelf. She handed them to her mother.

"I think that Eloise wants you to deliver these to Mr. Sierzik's room. She is frightfully busy." Sophia latched onto Rahzvon's arm and led him away.

"Sophia!" her mother objected.

Chapter XIII

"The Brother"

"A steed as black as the steeds of night
Was seen to pass as with eagle flight

As if he knew the terrible need
He stretched away with utmost speed"

—Thomas Buchanan Read

Refusing to make the delivery to Gaelon's room, Hannah sat them on the table. However, before long, her interest in the handsome guest, soon won out. She went to the hall for a quick check in the looking glass and carried the bouquet upstairs to the north wing. There, she saw Eloise exiting what she suspected to be Gaelon's assigned quarters. Eloise met her in the hall.

"They are lovely, mum. Go right in and place them on the table by the window," Eloise suggested grinning beneath her hand.

Hannah hesitated. She entered the room, slowly approaching the table when Gaelon appeared from behind the screen.

"You are a vision of beauty, like a bride coming down the aisle."

Hannah quickened her pace. "Thank you." She sat the vase in the center of the table.

"I thank you, Madame. I shall think of you every time I look at them."

"I prefer 'Hannah'. I should go now."

"Excuse me, *Hannah*, how well do you know my brother?"

"Honestly, I never trusted him from the first day that I met him. I realize, now, that I was somewhat irrational. You have to understand that when a mother finds that her daughter is obsessed with a man such as your brother..."

"Such as my brother?"

"He is...like you," she said bluntly.

Gaelon forced a smile. "I beg your pardon. What adverse opinion do you have, regarding Rahzvon and me?"

"I was only taken aback when I met Rahzvon; that is all. A mother imagines her daughter with a sweet young boy, not—. She *is* only nineteen."

"In Kosdrev, she would be the mother of three by now."

"This is not Kosdrev and I should be going."

"Would you take a walk with me after tea?"

Hannah glanced to the floor to avoid his irresistible smile and agreed, "Very, well." She walked confidently out to the hall. Gaelon nodded with a broad grin.

When Hiram and Livia arrived at the tentative site for the planned outing on Duncan Ridge, Hiram dismounted and helped Livia down from Duff.

"Hiram, it is prettier than I imagined. You can see for miles. I could stay here forever."

"Is that what you desire?"

"Of course. I would set up my tent, right here." She pointed to the ground. "Every time I awakened, I would look out over all of this and my day would be perfect." She spread out her arms and twirled around.

Hiram stepped in front of her with his arms folded across his chest and raised his chin presenting his profile. "All of this?"

Livia ignored his display. "I could bring the children up here. What a delightful place to run and play."

"*My* children?"

"I was not aware that you had any," she teased. "The children in my day school." Livia breathed the fresh air.

Hiram caught hold of her hand.

"Livy, I am serious. Would you want to live up here?"

"In a tent?"

"*Livy.* In a house—a bonnie house."

"Do you not think that the Duncans might object?"

"I doubt that their ghosts would take issue. This has not belonged to the Duncans in a century. This is all McDonnally ground that your wee feet stand upon."

"I must say that I am not surprised that you own your own piece of Heaven."

"The perfect residence for an angel."

"Why would you want to build a home up here when you have a beautiful estate?" She sat down on a boulder and crossed her ankles.

"It has no view and I never felt that it was actually mine. It is my father's."

"You are willing to give me such an extravagant gift?"

"It would be nothing in comparison to what you have done for me, love." He swept his hand across her hair and down her back.

"You would do almost anything for me, would you not, Hiram?"

"Aye," he kissed her neck.

"Then I want you to promise me that you will never lose your temper in my presence."

"Have I not demonstrated my control?" He took her hand and kissed it.

"I need your word."

He stepped back. "I sense a trap being set."

"Promise me, Hiram."

"I promise that I shall give it my best go."

"Hiram," she slid off the boulder and stood before him.

"Aye?" He grasped her shoulders and smiled down upon her.

In her sweetest voice she explained, "Your sister Hannah has invited Zedidiah Hartstrum to the McDonnally reunion."

Hiram's hands dropped to his sides as his dark eyes ignited.

"*Hiram,* you promised." She saw his fists clinch. "Hiram, remember your promise." She backed away. "I know that this does not please you, but your sister's life is her own. She obviously saw something redeeming in the man, which we did not."

Hiram stepped over to Duff.

"Hiram, what are you doing?"

"Come here, please."

"But, Hiram, we need to discuss this."

He helped her into the saddle and climbed on Hunter.

"Where are we going?" she asked fearfully.

"Home."

Hiram gave his horse a kick and galloped off. Livia followed knowing that she must act quickly. Hiram may have promised to keep his temper in her presence, but his fierce eyes promised quite the opposite for their return home.

Livia pulled back on the reins to halt Duff and jumped down. Hiram kept riding without notice, until several minutes later when agonizing over Livia's part in the matter, he turned back to look for her. She was nowhere to be seen. He steered Hunter back up over the hill to where he saw Livia standing next to her horse. Hiram rode hard and stopped next to Duff.

Seeing her reddened face, he quickly dismounted. "Livy, what has happened? Are you ill?"

"I do not know," she said short of breath.

He placed the back of his hand on her very warm, flushed face.

"Livy, you are on fire. You are having trouble breathing?" he said, panicking.

"I think that I need to sit," she said wearily.

"Hold on, love." Hiram quickly untied the rolled blanket behind his saddle, gave it a quick shake and spread it on the ground. "Let me help you." He carefully supported her waist while she sat. "Livy, I do not understand. Only a couple minutes past, you seemed well."

"It came over me...suddenly. You go on ahead. I know that you are in a hurry to get back to... to work on our kite design," she said faintly.

"I am not leaving you here." He gave her drink from the water flask. "I am worried about you, Livy." He sat down next to her and propped his arm behind her. "Here, lean on me."

"Thank you, Hiram. I am sorry—"

"Shh, you rest," he kissed the top of her head.

"I will be fine in a few minutes."

A minute passed and she sat up, "I am feeling better, now."

"Are you certain," he felt her forehead. "You seem to have cooled down."

"So have you," she mumbled.

"What Livy?"

She shook her head.

"Does this happen often, love?"

"Not often." *Only when I run laps around a horse*, she thought. She lowered her head shamefully. "Hiram, I feel terrible."

"I am taking you to Dr. Lambert, straight away." He scooped her up and placed her in Hunter's saddle. He pulled off Duff's bridle and gave him a smack. "Go home, Duff!" The horse took off like a shot toward the barn. Hiram climbed up behind her and wrapped one arm around her waist.

He tapped the reins gently against Hunter's neck to ease him forward.

"Stop!" Livia shrieked.

Hunter reared, but Hiram maintained his balance and cranked Hunter's head to the right to prevent him from bolting.

When the horse stopped, Livia broke free from Hiram's grasp and dropped to the ground.

"Livia what is wrong? Are you going to...to be sick?"

"No, no, no! I have behaved despicably. I should be horsewhipped!" she said pacing back and forth.

Hiram jumped from the saddle.

"Are you out of your head, lassie?"

"Yes, you might say that. I behaved like a lunatic woman, running circles around Duff!"

"You did *what?*"

Livia stopped pacing.

"Hiram, you are looking at a woman who has deceived you in the worst way. I purposely got myself overheated, to prevent you from returning home and raising all havoc over Hannah's invitation."

"Am I to understand that you are not ill? You never were?"

"Hiram, please forgive me. Do not look at me as though I was a common criminal."

"Livy, I was worried to *death* about you!"

"Do you not feel at ease...knowing that I am quite...fine?" she asked, grimacing.

Hiram scanned the ground angrily, digging his heal into the dirt. He walked over and climbed into the saddle.

"You are leaving me?" she asked pitifully. "Not that I would blame you."

He offered her his hand. "You shall regret that I did not." He lifted her up behind him.

"Hold on" were the last two words that she would hear from him for several hours to come. When they returned to his estate, Livia retired immediately to her room. Hiram retreated to his study. There he sat for several minutes and then began pacing for the next half hour.

An hour later, Livia met with Rahzvon, Sophia, Gaelon, and Hannah in the dining room for tea.

Eloise tapped at the study door, "Master, it is tea time."

"Thank you, Eloise. I shall be there directly."

"Yes, sir."

With everyone seated, Hiram entered the dining room and took his place at the head of the table.

"Good afternoon, Gaelon, Sophia, Rahzvon." He made contact with each, nodding in response. Hiram lowered his gaze, "Hannah."

"*Hiram,*" she responded, sensing his discontentment with her.

All eyes, except Hiram's regarded Livia with curiosity, waiting for Hiram's acknowledgement of her presence.

A moment later, he spoke sternly, "Livia."

Livia said nothing. *He never calls me Livia.*

Sophia was nearly exploding with curiosity as to the source of the rift between her uncle and Livia, but instead, found entertainment in extracting information about Gaelon and Rahzvon's childhood. Hiram and Livia listened with no comment.

When the meal ended, Gaelon discreetly met with Hannah in the garden; Rahzvon and Sophia retired to the parlor. Hiram and Livia remained at the table, neither wanting to make the first exit. Hiram finally left his chair.

"Livia, I would like to speak with you in my study," Hiram said in a parental tone.

She left her chair and placed her napkin on the table. Heavy with dread, she followed slowly, barely lifting her feet. When Hiram reached the doors to the study, he slid them open and waited for her like a guard at the dungeon.

Rahzvon and Sophia watched from across the hall, uncomfortably observing Hiram's serious expression. To their astonishment, Livia moved down the hall, on past the study, made the turn and started up the stairs. Hiram, shocked by her gumption, followed her to the second floor, after giving the onlookers a disapproving glare.

Hiram then summoned her, "Livia!"

She did not stop. She kept walking.

"Livia!"

She opened the door and entered her bedchamber. Hiram followed.

"Livy, I shan't be ignored under my own roof."

"I am not ignoring you—I am avoiding you."

"There is no difference, both are unacceptable."

Livia sat down on the bed. "Hiram, I am not going to stand for being berated for trying to become part of the family."

"You think acting with lunacy will make you a McDonnally?" he scorned.

Livia looked up with a mocking does-that really-sound-so-unreasonable look and shrugged.

Hiram clenched his teeth.

"Hiram, Edward was right. I was the only one with enough courage to inform you of Hannah's decision to invite Zed."

"Please, do *not* refer to him as, *Zed*." Hiram scowled. "*Edward?*"

"Yes, he suggested that I be the one to tell you."

"*Edward?*" his voice raised two notches. "That is why they invited you to Brachney Hall? That is why you nearly died of heat exhaustion? Stay here, until I return."

"*Hiram!* You promised!'" she called to him.

"Not to worry, you shan't be in my presence!"

He headed downstairs where Eloise had uncannily invited Naomi in the front entrance. Naomi raised her head at the sound of Hiram's boots hitting the stairs. When he appeared, his irritation was quite evident.

Naomi took a hold of Eloise's arm, "Eloise is the fabric in the kitchen," she asked hastily.

"Mum?"

"*Naomi.*" Hiram stepped next to her. "In the study!" he pointed.

Eloise gave Naomi a sympathetic pat on the hand as she followed him in.

Rahzvon and Sophia watched from the parlor, and then looked at one another as Hiram slammed the doors behind him.

"*Women,*" Rahzvon shook his head, empathizing with Hiram.

Sophia was not pleased with this one word comment and moved down to the opposite end of the divan.

"Naomi, Livy is *my* guest—Hannah is *my* sister! I cannot believe that you agreed to this abominable behavior! The two of you put my relationship with Miss Nichols in jeopardy."

Hiram moved in on her, "Were you aware that Livy nearly ran herself to death, because you forced her into telling me about that worm Hartstrum's invitation? She nearly fell faint, trying to keep me from returning home. She lied and deceived me! You should have seen her in that self-loathing state for her dishonesty!"

Naomi wrung her hands, "I warned Edward, but he would not listen to me. I had no part in it—I only invited her to tea." Naomi pleaded. "Hiram wait! "I shall go apologize to Livia!" she called as he burst from the study.

Naomi's hand covered her mouth at the blast of the doors banging into the pockets. She ran to the hall as Hiram blew through the main door. Naomi ran into the parlor.

"Rahzvon, please, stop him, Edward is in danger!"

Rahzvon left his chair and sprinted to the door.

"Wait!" Sophia called, chasing him. "Kiss me, I may never see you like this again!"

Rahzvon pulled her in and kissed her as though it were their last and was off.

Naomi steadied Sophia. "Pray for them—all of them."

After a moment of silence, excluding Sophia's swooning sighs, Naomi inquired as to which room was Livia's.

After a brief conversation, Livia openly accepted Naomi's apology.

Naomi suggested, "I think that our only solution is to keep Hiram distracted and a great distance from Zedidiah at all times."

"I agree. Given very little effort, I can be *very* distracting for Mr. McDonnally."

Naomi half smiled and raised her brows. Their immediate concern for Hiram and Edward overshadowed the problem with Zed's invitation and they returned to the parlor to wait.

Rahzvon followed Hiram who was moving rapidly in the direction of Brachney Hall. Rahzvon was grateful that Hiram was on foot, allowing time to diffuse his anger before he reached Edward's home.

Rahzvon caught up, "Mr. McDonnally, I need to speak with you," Rahzvon said breathing hard.

"Not now, Rahzvon." Hiram lengthened his stride.

"Sir, it is important. I need your advice."

"You have come to the wrong man. I offer no advice about women. I know nothing. Every day, I realize that I know even less."

Less than nothing? "Not about women—about my brother."

"What about him?" Hiram kept his vengeful pace.

"Gaelon wants to reconcile."

"I see no harm in that."

"But sir—he abandoned me."

"Water under the bridge. He is here for you now. Forgive him."

"Without a brother, you cannot understand."

"Nay, but Edward and I grew up as brothers."

"But the two of you have remained amiable."

"Not true. My move to Switzerland was due to a misunderstanding with Edward. I truly regret the lost years with him." Hiram slowed his pace. Rahzvon watched as Hiram stopped in the road, put his left hand on his hip and wiped the back of his right across his mouth. Hiram pondered as he squinted at Edward's home in the distance. A minute passed before he looked at Rahzvon, then back toward his home. The two men walked back to

McDonnally Manor. Neither spoke.

Gaelon walked around the fountain with Hannah at his side. "The meal was delicious," he said, sitting down on the edge of the fountain basin.

"Mrs. Zigmann is an excellent cook." Hannah said and joined him. "Gaelon, I have made a hasty decision. As an outsider, perhaps you can advise me. I have invited someone—a gentleman, to the family outing."

"Are you are having second thoughts?"

"Second, third, fourth. My brother had a serious confrontation with this gentleman."

"About you?"

"No, it was personal between them."

"May I ask why you would invite this man, knowing Hiram's difficulty with him?"

"After the confrontation, the gentleman approached me. He was extremely contrite for his rude behavior toward Hiram and begged my forgiveness and offered to apologize to Hiram."

"That is admirable."

"I thought that the family outing, would give Zed an opportunity to make amends, but now, I suspect Hiram is aware of the invitation and not pleased."

"I *suspect* that this apology was not the only source of motivation for the invitation—yours, or Zed's."

"I am the only woman without an escort."

"Hannah, this is a *family* event. It would be a grave mistake to invite this man. Notify Zed, that a brief written apology will suffice." He offered her his arm. They strolled toward the meadow.

"You need not worry about being the only woman without an escort."

"I shan't?"

"No, as a friend of the family, I might be convinced to take that position myself."

"Gaelon, would you do me the pleasure?"

"Porilt hiw ilsne." He grinned, "In other words, *I will think on it."*

Chapter XLV

"To Each His Own"

"Her gesture, motion
and her smiles.
Her wit, her voice,
my heart beguiles,"

—Thomas Ford

After the near confrontation with, Edward, Hiram went to Livia's room to finish speaking with her and knocked at her door.

"Who is it?"

"I."

Livia opened the door, "Good afternoon, Hiram."

"Take a turn around the grounds with me, please."

"Very well," Livia said cautiously.

They left the house and walked across the road to the meadow following the dirt path through the hills.

"Livy, what must you think? There has been nothing less than chaos since you arrived. First the school meeting, then the Kosdrev affair and now my sister's loss of sanity inviting that—"

"*Hiram.* Granted this life in Lochmoor Glen *is* considerably more colorful than mine was in London. But, as you said, I shall have to learn to accept it, if I am to remain here."

They walked on.

"Livy, I despise that you are afraid of me—of my temper."

"Are you anticipating a disturbance at the outing?"

"I shall keep my distance from *Mr.* Hartstrum... and his sharp tongue."

Livia gave a hopeful grin of approval and squeezed his arm.

"Livy, we are to be partners for the kite contest. I suggested croquet or cricket, but Edward nixed those. I suppose we should start working on our design," he said reluctantly.

"Have you ever made a kite?" Livia asked.

"I have constructed but one. Being a large man, I wanted my kite to be well-reinforced and over compensated a wee bit."

"Could not get it off the ground?"

"Nay. I apologize in advance—the day of the outing may prove to be one of great embarrassment for you."

"We need butcher paper, thin flexible trim sticks, paste, twine, and fabric strips."

Hiram stopped, staring at her inquisitively.

"Mr. McDonnally, your eyes rest upon the daughter of one of the world's greatest kite makers."

Hiram grinned ear-to-ear. "Ah, more proof that I have chosen the *perfect* woman." He lifted her from the ground and twirled her around.

Rahzvon and Sophia met in the barn to confer about their future masterpiece. Rahzvon took the horse crop, squatted down, and began to draw a design on the dirt floor.

"Phia, I think our kite should be shaped like this, so that it will support airlift." Sophia shuffled her feet across his sketch.

"Phia! What are you doing?"

"Please hand me the crop."

Rahzvon ground his teeth and handed it over.

Sophia drew an oval. "I want our kite to look like this—graceful with curves."

"We cannot build an oval kite." Rahzvon laughed and slid his boot through her drawing. He took the crop from her and redrew his original design while Sophia watched with growing frustration. He drew in the bracing and explained, "If my calculations are accurate, it should be about these proportions—twice as tall as it is wide."

Sophia asked for the crop. Rahzvon hesitated before surrendering it to her. She sat down and began adorning the sketch with a dozen flowers.

"Phia! You are destroying my plans. Now I cannot visualize the support system. Please, give me that; I have to redraw the braces and uproot this *garden.*"

Sophia's dark eyes burned. Rahzvon stood waiting with one hand on his hip and the other extended. Sophia whacked the crop across his hand.

"Ow!" He pulled his hand back and rubbed it.

"Design your own idiotic kite, Mr. Expert! I shan't be your accomplice!"

"*Assistant,* not accomplice," he corrected, checking his wound.

That remark sent Sophia into a destructive, wild, dance across Rahzvon's drawing followed by a triumphant march through the barn door.

In the Dugan shed, Tavy and Trina, too, sat sharing a tender moment over their kite proposals.

"Me thinks the kite should be designed like a mainsail," Tavy said with his arm over Trina's shoulders.

"But, Tavy, sails are anchored to the ship, they are not meant to fly," Trina said sweetly.

"Aye, cloth is perfect."

"I should think that it would be too heavy," she said cautiously.

Tavy lowered his arm and stood in front of her. "Trina, on a ship, there's but one captain. That would be me. Yer the first mate."

Trina stood up, "Henry McTavish, this is not a ship and I demand equal rights."

"Equal rights for a woman on a ship?"

"Forget it! I shall make my own!" Trina ran from the shed.

"Mutiny!" Tavy called after her.

Guillaume and Allison sat on the back step of the cottage holding hands.

"Allison, I do not want you to worry about the kite competition, my dearest."

"You are so thoughtful." She kissed his cheek.

"I shall be handling it. You go and enjoy yourself, knitting or something."

Allison removed her hand from his. "But Guillaume, this is a partnership. We are to work together, like Rahzvon and Sophia and the others."

"Ah, but one brain is better than two in our situation, love. Remember, *I* am the architect," he boasted.

"Guillaume, we are not preparing plans for a bridge or a building. I have some ideas for the kite, too."

"Allison, do not be silly. You know nothing of aerodynamics," he laughed.

"Laugh at me—you shall see! I shall make my own kite! Your mother was right, 'smart women love foolish men!'"

"Do not let my father hear you say that!"

Allison disappeared around the side of the cottage where she saw Trina storming across the pasture from the Dugans' and Sophia pacing in the garden. Allison recognized the symptoms.

"Trina, wait!" Allison called.

Trina shook her head, "That bull-headed sailor has to do everything his way."

"Guillaume refused to even discuss the plans for our kite. He is designing it by himself, because he is the *architect*," she scorned.

Allison and Trina opened the gate to the garden to join Sophia.

"Is Rahzvon being as unreasonable as our partners?" Trina asked.

"Worse, I imagine. You should have seen him stomping all over my flowers. All I wanted was a few decorations on our kite."

Allison and Trina nodded sympathetically.

"Ladies, I think we need to create our own entry. Agreed?" Allison asked.

"Agreed!" Sophia and Trina shouted.

"Do either of you know anything about kites?" Allison inquired.

They shook their heads.

"Then we need assistance." Allison pondered when she and Sophia came to the realization simultaneously.

"Jake Kilvert!"

"He made it to the kite finals in Glasgow," Sophia explained. "Come on, I shall summon a driver to take us to the livery to speak with him."

Edward sat in his library preparing two lists: one for kite materials, the other for the stew ingredients.

"Busy, love?" Naomi entered the room with two cups of tea.

"Thanks to my loving wife, *very* busy."

"I may have suggested the stew, but your crew decided on the kites."

"Naomi, I am feeling somewhat guilty about the kite contest. We promised to treat Hiram with greater respect. I do not relish the idea of seeing him humiliated again in Livia's presence. His kite expertise is severely limited."

"For the time being, I suggest you say very little to Hiram and Livia. Hiram was irate about the suggestion for Livia to bear the ill-tidings of Zed's invitation."

"Oh well, Hiram is aware that it was *your* idea," Edward said with satisfaction.

"*No*, Edward, your idea. It was embarrassing. I had to grovel to Livia. It was not at all pleasant."

"What is my nephew planning to do with the unwanted guest? Throw him into the pond?"

"You are fortunate that he has not chosen to throw you in."

Edward leaned back in his chair. "Great Scott, can we not have one normal McDonnally event?"

"Apparently not."

The day for the outing was nothing less than perfect; there was no rain in sight and a gentle breeze to accommodate the contest. However, due to the inconvenience of transporting the tents, food, table, chairs, and the like, the site of the outing was relocated behind Edward and Naomi's estate, near the pond.

The Wheaton children were ecstatic, despite their earlier disappointment in finding that Marvin and Conrad, Naomi and Edward's nephews, would not be attending. Pearl, their mother, was ill and not up to the trip. The girls found solace in making small kites for decorations, which Naomi had nailed to wooden stakes lining the shore of the pond. The women donned their most colorful attire and the men wore casual white shirts. The group assembled by the pond promptly at two o'clock.

The guests were welcomed with a number of cheery Scottish tunes performed by Albert on fiddle and Naomi on her zither. Edward made one last taste check of his stew, and then sat at a table inside the tent to take charge of the kite registration. Eloise assisted the Brachney Hall cook in organizing the tables displaying the food.

Hiram and Livia arrived, surprised to find that the younger men and women congregated in opposing sides of the yard. From the exchange of glares between the gender groups, a dispute between them was obviously responsible. Hiram and Livia split up to investigate the unfavorable situation.

Hiram approached the men, "Are we having a problem with our ladies?"

"Allison is ridiculous! Can you imagine her telling me, the architect, how to design a kite?" Guillaume said with disgust.

"Rahzvon?"

"I beg your pardon, sir, but your niece is the most stubborn, irrational woman who I have ever met."

"She is a McDonnally," Hiram said calmly.

Hiram looked at Tavy. "And Miss Dunmore?"

"She mayna be a McDonnally, but Joseph's mule would hae been a more suitable partner."

"I see that you and Livia remain thick as thieves," Rahzvon noted.

"Aye, my woman knows who is in control." Hiram grinned and walked away.

The huddling women greeted Livia.

"Hello, Livia," Allison said looking over her shoulder at the conspiring men.

"Good afternoon. Are you prepared for the contest?"

"We certainly are. The men did not take a fancy to working with us, so we made our own kite," Sophia smiled smugly, watching Rahzvon.

"Indeed?" Livia glanced down at their entry hidden beneath paper wrapping.

"Did Hiram bully you, too?" Trina asked.

"Not at all. Perhaps it is because he is older and wiser."

"I shan't believe that Rahzvon shall ever accept me as an equal," Sophia complained.

"Guillaume either...as long as he is providing the income," Allison scowled.

"And your sailor, Trina?" Livia looked toward Tavy who was standing as tall and as proud as the rest of his comrades.

"Henry McTavish is a sailor. That says it all. I was forced to abandon ship."

Livia laughed. "My friends, keep in mind that this outing was planned as a reunion, not as a battlefield. Good luck." She waved and met with Hiram at the registration table.

"Learn anything of the dispute?" Livia asked.

"Nothing specific, but they were curious as to how we resolved our issues."

"What did you tell them, Hiram?"

"My exact words were, *my woman knows who is in control.*"

"You could not have explained it more accurately." Livia grinned.

They stopped at the registration table. Seeing Hiram and Livia empty-handed, Edward asked sympathetically, "Ah, no kite, Hiram?"

"Nay, we have an entry." Hiram beamed.

"Much smaller, this time, eh? Where is it, in your pocket?" Edward chuckled. Hiram's disturbed expression warranted Edward's retreat. "Uh... no harm meant, Hiram."

"We will present it when the contest begins," Livia explained.

"You do realize that the two of you, and Naomi and myself, are the only couples with a joint entry?"

"Pity," Hiram said gazing across at the warring couples.

The Wheaton children were floating sailboats along the shoreline, when Marvel spotted Hiram. She handed her string to Corinne and ran to him.

"Mr. McDonnally!"

"Marvel."

"Thank ya, sir, for speakin' to Mr. McDonnally 'bout the stamp album. He was understandin', just as ya said."

"My pleasure, Miss Wheaton. Now, remember, no playing with the lanterns and no more late night excursions." He looked to Sophia remembering her night in the woods with Rahzvon. "After dark, you stay in the house."

Edward left his table and picked up the megaphone. "Fetch your kites. The contest is about to begin. The contestant with the entry remaining in the air the longest, shall win the grand prize!"

Sophia turned to Rahzvon and stuck out her tongue. He narrowed his eyes and pointed a warning finger at her.

Sophia, Trina and Allison carefully removed the wrapping from their kite while Naomi went into the house to get theirs. Livia and Hiram disappeared into the tool shed. While everyone was detangling their string and making the final check, Hiram and Livia took the opportunity to enjoy their privacy.

Livia pulled the white sheet from their simple, but enormous kite.

"*Voilla!*" she exclaimed.

"Magnificent, Livy. I could not have done it without you."

"Correction, love. You could not have done it at all."

"Come here my little genius for your reward."

"Hiram, there are windows in this shed."

"Let them watch. Maybe our kiss will be contagious and the feud will fizzle out. How long has it been, Livy?"

"More hours than I can bear," she laughed and slid her fingers through his beard. Hiram danced her over to the wall. "Hiram, what are you doing?"

"I am positioning us in front of the window. They need encouragement. Besides, there shall be a great need for consoling after the contest and it shan't be ours."

"Hiram, stop! This is embarrassing."

Despite Livia's playful objection to his advances, the kiss was romantic and very lengthy for the benefit of the audience, as well as the participants. No one intended to intrude on their privacy, but Hiram and Livia's absence was delaying the contest. Sophia, Trina, and Allison observed the interlude envying Livia's positive relationship with her partner. The young men watched, definitely having second thoughts about offering a truce to their lovely opponents. Rahzvon had difficulty keeping his distance from Sophia since that first day when they met. Guillaume missed Allison's gentle protective ways and Tavy feared losing the only woman who shared a mutual interest in him. Hannah and Gaelon kept a watchful eye on the children by the pond. Hannah, having lived in Paris, did not understand the fascination with the amorous scene, but found herself considering the possibilities with her handsome escort. She peeked up at Gaelon, re-evaluating his appearance. She decided that he was every bit as handsome as Rahzvon and definitely much more appealing than Zedidiah Hartstrum.

Naomi and Edward were engaged in an argument over the knots in their string, ignoring the rendezvous, while Beatrice peered at a carriage in the drive. Expecting to see Daniel emerge, she was quite surprised to see a stranger climb out and walk toward the party.

"Edward, who is that gentleman?" Beatrice asked.

Edward was floored. His nephew had ignored his advice and invited his accountant, George Hicks, as an escort for Hannah.

"Edward, good to see you."

"George, welcome."

"I do not see Hiram and one can always spot him," George laughed.

"Hiram is...right there." He pointed toward the shed where Livia and Hiram were vacating their retreat. Edward did a double take when he saw Hiram withdrawing the giant kite. "Oh, Hiram, not again." He sighed. "Big man has to have a big kite," he mumbled.

The *oohs* and *ahhs* from the children seeing the massive kite, put the other competitors on guard.

Edward turned to George. "You arrived in time for the kite competition."

Chapter XV

"Turn Tail and Run"

"Kind jealous doubts,
tormenting fears,
And anxious cares,
when past,
Prove our heart's treasure
Fixed and dear,
And make us blest at last"

—John Wilmot

The children agreed to hold the kites while the contestants positioned to run with the strings. Jeanie insisted on holding Rahzvon's and Marvel struggled with Hiram and Livia's. Once everyone was in position, Albert shot his pistol to begin the event. The contestants ran and three of the six kites were airborne. Allison, Trina and Sophia screamed with delight as their floral creation lifted off. Guillaume's architectural phenomenon ricocheted behind him across the meadow until it was decimated into a dozen pieces. Tavy's "sail" broke free and floated off to land, at home in the pond, while Naomi and Edwards kite made a quick u-turn and dive-bombed into the ground and split in two.

During the demolition, Hiram and Livia's monster climbed steadily. Rahzvon's kite was sheer entertainment for the spectators, as it would loop several times before spiraling downward. Rahzvon's quick control kept it aloft. Sophia, Allison and Trina took turns handing off their controlling spool. They were thoroughly delighted with their success and had no qualms about displaying it.

Tavy and Guillaume were determined that the best man should win and ran to cheer on their comrade, Rahzvon. The Wheaton girls squealed with joy running beneath the looming ornaments and the baby Dara clapped her hands, focused on the giant kite that dwarfed the remaining two. All watched intently to see which would be the next to be lost. Nearly fifteen minutes passed before Rahzvon's string became taut as the winds increased.

"I am going to lose it!" Rahzvon yelled.

Gaelon called out to him, "Give her some slack, brother!" Rahzvon let out the remaining string, which temporarily ameliorated his dilemma.

The young women danced around proudly

with their spool as their kite waltzed with them. Unfortunately, their lack of attention put their kite in immediate danger of becoming prey to the only tree in the meadow—the mighty oak. Within seconds, the tree took their kite prisoner, sending its creators into a frenzy. Then, there was a melancholy moment of silence.

Hiram stood proudly with his one arm around Livia, the other guiding their prized example of cooperation. Sophia watched the two remaining entries, debating where her loyalty should lie. Rahzvon's little kite fluttered merrily, seldom still, where Hiram's looked as though someone had pasted it up in the sky; only the tail showed any sign of movement. Sophia watched Hiram leisurely controlling his, while Rahzvon fought numerous downdrafts, determined to plummet his to the ground. Then Rahzvon started to lose his again.

"It's going!" he yelled.

Gaelon shouted, "Run backwards, Rahzvon!"

Sophia could not help herself, "Run, Rahzvon, run!"

Rahzvon turned to see Sophia jumping up and down. His momentary pleasure in seeing her display of support was enough distraction for him to lose all control. His kite came crashing downward.

The crowd *ohhed* with disappointment. All regarded the giant beauty still hovering majestically, releasing only an occasional rippling sound of its paper.

Edward picked up the megaphone. "Much to my surprise, my nephew, Hiram, and his lovely partner, Livia, are the grand prize winners for this year's kite competition!"

Everyone clapped and cheered. Hiram leaned down and kissed his partner. They were greeted with an even louder applause.

"What's the prize, Mr. Donnally?" Jeanie's little voice called out.

"The prize is a three day holiday at Deeside for two!"

Hiram's dimples vanished with the announcement. Deeside was the location Hiram had chosen for the surprise honeymoon for Abigail. In his shock to the announcement, Hiram inadvertently let go of the kite string and the winning entry drifted away towards his home, ending the applause. With Guillaume leading, the Wheaton girls screamed and went chasing and grasping for the tail.

Livia looked up with concern, "Hiram, do you disapprove of the prize?"

Seeing Livia's disappointment, and with two hands now free, Hiram embraced her. "Nay, Livy. I was only surprised at Edward's generosity." He waved at Edward, "We thank you!"

"You earned it!" Edward replied. "Let us eat!"

Hiram saw George talking to Beatrice and took Livia over to introduce her.

"Livia Nichols, what a surprise!" George took her hand and kissed it.

Hiram stood with marked confusion.

"Good afternoon, George. How are you?" Livia asked.

"Very well, thank you. I thought that I would never see you without Thomas clinging to you. I see Hiram is the fortunate fellow, now."

Thomas? Hiram looked down at Livia with discontent eyes. Livia avoided them and took George's arm too.

"Shall we get something to eat?" Livia asked sweetly.

"Who is Thomas?" Hiram whispered in Livia's ear, while she held her bowl for Eloise to fill.

"No one."

"*Livy.*"

Allison and Trina bounded over to Livia and moved in between her and Hiram.

"Livia, we need to speak with you. Come on." They took her arms and whisked her away.

"Very well, do not tell me," Hiram muttered. "I shall find out on my own." He sat down at the small table across from George Hicks.

"Hiram, is that your twin, Hannah?" George observed the couple seated on the blanket.

"Aye, George. Who is Thomas?"

"Old chap, let sleeping dogs lie."

"I have a right to this information. Livy and I are to be married."

"Congratulations. In that case, Livia should be given the opportunity to tell you herself."

"George, when did you become so righteous? I do not like your tone. You are implying that this man was significant in her life."

"Hiram, I am your accountant, not your social advisor. What is your worry, man? You and Livia seem to have a strong relationship. Past encounters should have no bearing on it." George took a bite, swallowed and then asked, "Who is the man with your sister? I thought I was to be her escort."

"He is a son of a late friend. Tell me the man's line of business."

George shook his head. "No, that would not be a good idea. Just forget it Hiram and enjoy your holiday."

"George, I demand that you tell me or you are sacked."

"Hiram, do not be absurd. Ask Livia. She will tell you."

"Why has she not told me before?"

"She probably thought that it was un-important. I am going for a piece of carrot cake. Do you want some?"

Hiram did not reply and left the area in search of Livia. Beatrice stopped him midway.

"Hiram, Daniel never arrived. I am worried."

"When was he to come?"

"Hours ago."

"Anything is possible—a delay with the train, a broken wheel on his cart. You stop worrying. If we do not see him by nightfall, I shall check into it. He is on a well-travelled road. Now enjoy your holiday," he repeated George's sentiment.

Hiram saw Livia with the women. As he approached the group, he heard them interrogating Livia about her contribution to the winning entry. Hiram gently took her arm and led her away to the pond. "Excuse me, ladies."

"Hiram, where are we going? I should like a piece of carrot cake," Livia said innocently.

"Livia Nichols, I want a straight answer. Who is Thomas?"

Livia faced Hiram, "Who is Elizabeth?"

"I am asking the questions. "Who is this Thomas and where and when did you meet him?"

"Who is Allison, who is Naomi, and who is Abigail, *Hiram*? Did I ask you about the details of your relationships?"

"No, you just tried to run away. I am not going anywhere, so I suggest that you tell me about this Thomas character."

"That is exactly what he is."

"What?"

"A character."

"Please, do not be insolent with me, Livy."

"I am not. He was a character in a play—an actor."

"An actor? What kind of actor?"

"My leading man, if you must know. Are you quite satisfied? Now, I am going for my cake."

"Why have you never spoken of him?"

"History, Hiram. He is part of insignificant history. Now, please step aside."

"George insinuated that you and this man were inseparable," Hiram prodded.

"Hiram, that was years ago at a summer theater production. We spent a lot of time working together—that is all. Now, may I get a piece of cake before it is gone?"

"How close were you working together?"

"That is the last straw, Hiram McDonnally! I shan't be badgered any longer. I am going for my cake!"

Hiram blocked her path. "You are staying."

"I am not."

Hiram stepped closer; Livia stepped back.

"Move out of my way, Hiram."

Hiram shook his head and stepped another step toward her.

Livia stepped back. "You seem to think that because you are twice my size, you can bully me."

"Aye, I do."

"Perhaps, I should call for assistance."

"The choice is yours, Livy."

She stepped back again. Hiram stepped forward.

"Hiram, you are being a nuisance. Please, move."

"Never. I would not take another step, if I were you. Your next shall land you in the pond."

"Hiram, what do you think you shall accomplish by detaining me?" Livia put her hands on her hips.

"I shall have your undivided attention and a few honest answers."

"Does it feed your ego, to trap me here like a helpless animal?"

"You are anything, but helpless, Livy." Now what shall I ask first," he folded his arms.

Livia made a break for it—but Hiram's quick hands returned her to her position. "Were you in love with him?"

"No. I liked him, a great deal."

Hiram scowled. "Did he kiss you—acting or otherwise?"

"No, Hiram."

"Hmm? Did you enjoy our time in the shed?"

Livia hesitated with the unexpected question. "Yes."

"Do you have any other men in your past?"

"*Hiram.*"

"An answer, Livy."

"Hiram! I want my cake, now."

"Can you swim, Livy?"

"You would not dare?" She shrank back.

"Aye, I would and as you know, I always tell the truth. Tell me, Livy."

Livia laughed nervously, "Hiram, the pond is cold."

"Aye, tell me, are there any others?"

"I refuse to be bullied."

"I warned you." Hiram gently knocked her off balance. She fell into the pond with a scream. Hiram burst out laughing, while she swam out from the shore.

She called back to him, "Did I tell you about Stephen, my father's bodyguard, or Pablo, my Italian teacher?"

Hiram cocked his head objectionably, pulled off his boots, and dove in after her.

Livia swam towards the opposite shore.

"Faster, Livia," Trina and Sophia cheered her on. "Remember women's rights!"

To the dismay of her female companions, Livia was a good swimmer, but no match for Hiram. He caught up with her in less than a minute. Livia's attempt to escape was painless. The two ended up sitting on the opposite bank in each other's arms. The surrender was a pleasant one with Turkish towels provided by the attending servants.

"Livy, tell me the truth. Who did you fall in love with after you left Switzerland?"

"Let me see...ah yes. It was at the Seattle Exposition—the World's Fair, 1904."

"Impossible, the World's Fair was held in St. Louis that year."

"Hiram McDonnally, you astonish me."

"I am aware that there is a world outside the British Isles."

"Well, no matter, that was the year that I met my true love, the year father and I were to go yachting with Cornelius on the *North Star*."

Hiram sat up. "You fell in love with Cornelius Vanderbilt?"

"You know how I feel about wealthy men," she said coyly.

"Where did you meet him?" Hiram grumbled.

"In New York."

"And how did you find his residence, Livy?"

"His residence?"

"Yes, his home?" Hiram asked keenly.

"Nice...large."

"Where is that located, again?"

"On Fifth Avenue."

"Ah yes, near 92nd Street."

"Yes, 92nd," Livia quickly agreed.

Hiram threw his head back and laughed. "Livy, you may confess now."

"What?"

"Mr. Vanderbilt's black, long townhouse is located between 42nd and 57th. Andrew Carnegie's home is on 92nd."

"Oh... yes."

"Of course, you are familiar with Jay Gould, up the street, Livy."

Livia grinned. "Of course, he only inherited just short of eighty million," she said confidently.

Hiram was silenced.

Trina and Sophia walked back to the refreshment table to sample the fruit.

"Watching Uncle Hiram and Livia makes me wish that Rahzvon would come to his senses," Sophia said choosing a small sprig of grapes.

"Tavy's absence is beginning to wear on me, too," Trina agreed.

"Trina, men see no need for apologies, like we do. If we are ever to be objects of their admiration, I think that we may have to inspire them to relent."

"What are you scheming, Sophia?" Trina asked suspiciously. "Allison went over to Guillaume and behaved as though nothing was wrong. Should we do the same?"

"Absolutely not, Trina. A woman should have her pride. They shall come to us. Do as I do," Sophia instructed. Sophia backed casually over to the side of the tent where Tavy and Rahzvon were eating their cake on the other side.

Sophia spoke loudly, "Trina, was it not marvelous how Rahzvon handled his kite?"

Trina was perplexed at first, but caught on quickly. "Oh, yes, he is very talented when it comes to taking control."

Rahzvon looked up, listening to the favorable conversation.

Sophia confirmed, "Yes, he is not a man to bend to another's demands."

"Tavy's kite was beautiful—do you not think so, Sophia? Trina added.

Tavy looked up from his cake to Rahzvon.

"Yes, much too beautiful to fly. Did you see the Celtic cross painted on it?" Sophia asked. "It is refreshing to know a man of such high religious values," Sophia pointed out.

"Compassionate men are rare. Yes, Henry may have a tough exterior, but inside he is a loving, gentle man," Trina pointed out.

Sophia then motioned to Trina. "I give them about thirty seconds." The excited women walked briskly away from the tent and split up. Sophia walked over to Beatrice, who was uncommonly forlorn over Daniel's absence, and Trina ran to help Jeanie who was trying to fix her toy boat. Rahzvon and Tavy gave each other knowing grins, shoved down the last bites, and left to search for their women.

Beatrice relayed her fears to Sophia for Daniel's welfare, until Sophia agreed to talk to Hiram about an investigation of Daniel's disappearance. Rahzvon watched from the horseshoe pits. He found Sophia's animated appearance to be intriguing and entertaining. He eyed her attractive dress for the first time that day. The bright red fabric accented her black curls. She was beautiful and he felt that he had spent entirely too much time away from her.

Sophia spoke with Hiram and walked in the opposite direction from where Rahzvon was watching. He did not hesitate and like a horse following a carrot on a stick, he moved steadily behind her to the hill toward the end of the pond. Her slow stroll gave him the opportunity to catch up with her.

"May I join you?" he asked.

She turned as though she was surprised, "*Rahzvon,* why yes."

"It has been an interesting day."

"Yes, the contest was extilerating. I am sorry that you did not win."

Rahzvon was very tempted to correct her mispronunciation, but was not about to upset her in any way. "Thank you, Phia."

"I thought that it was especially nice that your brother offered you advice."

"I *was* surprised that Gaelon took an interest. May we sit down over there?" He pointed to a grassy knoll.

"If you like." Sophia sat and straightened her skirt. "There are certainly going to be a lot of dirty dishes."

Rahzvon laughed, "Yes, there are."

"My servants shall never have to wash dishes."

"No?"

"No, I spent too many hours over a steaming sink at the café. I would not wish that on anyone."

"What are they going to do? Throw the dishes away and buy new ones?"

"No silly. I shall have an automated dishwasher."

"A what?"

"Livia told me all about them. She saw them at the World's Fair. I told Eloise about them, so that she could request Uncle Hiram, to purchase a few."

"You amaze me, Phia. You could be Britain's Alice Roosevelt—so determined, full of life and unpredictable with all the charm of a princess—well not Creazna."

"That is very nice of you to say, Rahzvon."

"Phia, you look beautiful today," He stroked her cheek.

"Only today?"

"Every day. Are you still angry with me?" he asked.

"Should I be?"

"No. I have something to ask you, Phia."

"Rahzvon, are you not going to kneel?" she asked anxiously.

"Not that, not yet."

"What then?" she asked, disappointed.

"Gaelon has asked me to become a partner in his business."

"That is grand!" She looked at him with questioning eyes, "But that is not a question."

"You are very perceptive, Little One."

"I think *attentive* would be the correct word," she said coolly. "Rahzvon, if you are asking my permission, I—"

"Phia, I would never ask your permission." He quirked a brow and turned away from her. "What would you think if I were to spend much of my time travelling to various countries?"

"Your time? You meant to say our time."

Rahzvon turned back to her secure expression. "It is necessary for the job, Phia."

"Positively perfect. I long to see the other side of the world," she said confidently.

"I have not inquired as to whether or not it would be acceptable to bring you with me."

"I suggest that you do...*inquire*, immediately. I have no desire to remain in a relationship with only a handful of letters to amuse me," she said regarding him boldly.

"Phia, I never agreed to take the job," he said defensively.

"You considered it."

Rahzvon took her hand, his gaze moving up her arm to meet her resentful eyes. He displayed the *look*—the one that never failed to extinguish her anger. His lips parted slightly as he watched Sophia's defenses fighting to resist his alluring charm. She weakened within his arms.

"Little One, do you really believe that I could leave you?" he whispered and kissed her neck.

"I should...I should hope not," she replied. Her heart raced as he kissed the other side of her neck. "Does this mean that I am going...going with you?" She closed her eyes as he kissed her cheek.

"It means that we are never," he kissed her other cheek, "ever, arguing again." Before she had a chance to respond, her attention was diverted by the kiss from a man who had been deprived of her attention for one too many hours.

Chapter XVI

"God's Will"

"God moves in a mysterious way
His wonders to perform;
He plants his footsteps in the sea,
And rides upon the storm."

—William Cowper

Trina tied the little cord that fastened the mainsail to Jeanie's sailboat.

"Trouble wit' yer mainsail, matey?" Tavy asked standing over them.

"Aye, captain," Jeanie saluted.

"Yer in good hands. Me first mate has made an expert repair." He placed a hand on Trina's shoulder.

"Thank ye, captain."

Jeanie took the boat from Trina and placed it in the water. Trina stood up and gave Tavy a shy smile. Jeanie pointed to Tavy's kite floating on the surface in the center of the pond.

"What 'bout yer kite, captain? Better rescue it."

"Not a bad idea, matey," he answered, ready to match the powerful swimming skills that Hiram demonstrated earlier. He wasted no time in removing his boots and shirt. By Trina's expression, it was obvious that she was not only astonished, but also successfully impressed. The encouraged sailor dove in and swam in perfect form to the center of the pond. When he returned to shore with his kite, Trina attempted to get a second look at the unusual tattoo on his shoulder blade. She sidestepped for a closer look when he pulled on his shirt. Tavy basked in the attention of her wandering eyes.

A few yards away, Guillaume watched Trina's obsessive attention to the sailor. He turned to Allison, "Do you think that I should get a tattoo?"

Allison broke into uncontrollable laughter. Guillaume scowled indignantly.

Allison finally regained control, in seeing his disapproval. "I am sorry, dear, but," she took his hand, "Guillaume, I prefer a man with a brilliant mind."

Her compliment helped his ego immensely, but he did not hesitate in leading Allison a good distance from the pond and from his massive, drenched friend. However, the impressive sailor, lacking in the social graces, was at a loss as what to do next.

"Would ye be desirin' a piece o' cake, Trina?" he asked awkwardly.

"No, thank you."

"Fruit?"

"No, I have had quite enough to eat."

Fortunately, for the inexperienced young man, Naomi and Albert found their instruments and resumed their playing. Tavy looked around and then stepped closer to Trina. "If ye dunna mind a wee bit o' water...would ye join me in this dance?"

Trina's smile was an adequate answer. Henry McTavish, large, unrefined man that he was, proved to be light on his feet. He spun Trina smoothly around the meadow. Their rhythmic grace inspired the other couples to join in. Gaelon sprinted over to Hannah, interrupting her conversation with George Hicks, and swept her away. Hiram's preoccupation with Gaelon's intervention, forced Livia to request an invitation.

"Mr. McDonnally, are you not going to ask me to dance? Or do you prefer a water ballet?"

Hiram ignored her inquiry. "Have I told you how bonnie you look today, Miss Nichols?"

"No you have not and if you do, I shan't waste hours preparing to meet with you again," she laughed, primping her damp hair and straightening her wrinkled dress.

"It would be a waste, when you could spend those hours with me in your natural state of beauty. Come, dance with me, my water goddess."

Soon the estate was dotted with whirling couples. In watching Naomi perform, Edward saw the little figure of Jeanie Wheaton in the distance focused on Rahzvon and Sophia sharing a kiss as they waltzed. Edward felt that it was his duty to distract the little girl and ran to her side.

"Miss Wheaton would you give me the honor of this dance?"

Jeanie looked up through her tears of jealousy. "Aye, sir," she sniffled.

Edward whisked her away, nearer to the musicians' platform. He reached down to lead. The great difference in their height was soon resolved when Edward lifted Jeanie from the ground and continued moving gracefully in large circles around the other participants. Very soon, Jeanie had forgotten about Rahzvon, and was laughing wildly with each breathtaking spin.

Fair weather and good humor blessed the afternoon outing, until a messenger boy pedaled his red bicycle onto the estate in search of the McDonnally men. As the evening drew to a close, the servants arrived to pack up the remaining food and dishware. During the lowering of the tents and the removal of the tables and chairs, the guests mingled for a while longer, before the summer sunset. The messenger located Hiram speaking with Hannah and George Hicks. He handed Hiram the wire.

"This is for ya, sir."

"Thank you, lad." Hiram handed him a few coins. "Go on into the house and tell them that Hiram sent you to enjoy a piece of carrot cake."

"Thank ya, sir! First I hae a delivery for yer uncle."

"Aye? Be on your way." He turned to Hannah and George, "Excuse me."

Hiram sat down on the bench attached to the tool shed and opened the wire. Before reading it, he glanced to the bottom of the page, in search of the sender's name. *Daniel.*

He eagerly began reading.

HIRAM——CONFIDENTIAL.
RECOVERING IN IRELAND FROM ATTACK BY CECIL'S MEN IN ATTEMPT TO GAIN INFORMATION OF BEATRICE'S RESIDENCE. REMAINED SILENT. ME SHOPPE BURNED TO THE GROUND. JEREMIAH AND FAMILY FLED TO WALES. APOLOGIZE TO BIRDIE. TELL HER I SHALL SEE HER SOON. DO NOT GET INVOLVED,

DANIEL

Hiram stood up, shocked and outraged. He could not fathom the pain and injustice his dearest friend had suffered. He began breathing hard as every bone in his body felt the need to retaliate. His world went dark, blinded to the jovial atmosphere surrounding him. His black eyes, filled with hate searched the landscape for a place to release his erupting anger. He instinctively turned and stormed into the shed, crushing the cryptic note in his right fist, which immediately met the wall with incredible force. His bellow in gisaleon sent Livia running toward the scene.

Hiram wearing the crazed expression of a rabid dog, pulled his hand from the wall as Livia entered.

"Hiram, your hand! What has happened?" she panicked.

He fell against the table and slowly opened his bleeding hand, staring at the paper.

"*Hiram?*"

His injured hand moved to cover his tear-filled eyes, Livy's hands trembled as she tried to comfort him. He tried to collect his thoughts, but the vision of Daniel's battered body and the decimated shop were debilitating. He did not move, and then exclaimed, "I cannot believe this has happened. Blast it!"

"Hiram, you are frightening me."

"I need to speak with Beatrice."

"*Hiram?*" Livia did not pursue her line of questioning. She knew Hiram well enough to understand that he would share the information when he was ready. Fearful of the origin of his pain and anger, and knowing the common interest with Beatrice was most likely Daniel, Livy watched Hiram enter the house.

Hiram found Beatrice in the hall.

"Beatrice, may I speak with you in the library?"

"Yes, but, your hand. What happened? You are bleeding." She grimaced at his mangled knuckles.

"Showing off my strength," he forced a grin and led her into the room.

"Beatrice, I know that you have been worried about Daniel, but I just received word from him."

"Yes?" She wrung her hands.

"Good news. Daniel sends his apologies and shall be seeing you very soon."

"Is that all?"

Hiram despised withholding the information, but honored Daniel's wish. "And he really wanted to be here today, but unexpected circumstances altered his plans."

"I understand. He is very busy with the shoppe. I am thankful that he is well; that is all that is important. Thank you, Hiram. Now let me help you with that hand, come along."

Hiram followed her back to the kitchen pantry where she gathered the necessary items to clean and bandage his hand.

"Hiram, I hope that the person on the receiving end of this fist does not need my assistance."

Hiram tried to smile. "Nay."

Livia entered the kitchen and moved quickly toward them. Hiram's forbidding gaze met hers, as he gave a subtle headshake.

"I was just telling Beatrice, how my ego got the best of me in the challenge," Hiram explained.

Livia nodded, "Ah, yes, men will be men," she muttered.

"Young lads who never grow up," Beatrice agreed.

When she finished, Hiram thanked her and she left to gather the children. Without further discussion of the incident, Hiram and Livia returned to the yard, where George Hicks approached them and offered a handshake. Hiram declined.

"I hurt it in the shed."

"Ah, sorry, man. Now, I thank you, Hiram, for the invitation. I found it all to be quite interesting. I hope to meet with your lovely sister, Hannah, very soon." He gave Hiram a wink. Already disturbed with Daniel's situation, Hiram found George's confident air unsettling, and he regretted providing the invitation.

After George made his exit, Gaelon moved into stake his claim on Hiram's twin.

"Hannah, I have thoroughly enjoyed myself today and I attribute this to not only the time spent in my brother's company, but to your presence."

"That is very kind of you, Gaelon."

"I know that it has been a long day, but are you up to a walk back to the manor?"

"Gaelon, I am a woman who has spent nineteen hours a day on her feet for nearly sixteen years. A leisurely walk home would not bother me in the least." She took his arm.

Edward stood on the back step directing traffic. While the last chair was carried into the house, he opened and read the wire. He looked up with a heavy heart and stuffed it into his pocket. He scanned the yard for Naomi and saw her laughing with Beatrice as they were herding the uncooperative girls into the house.

"Sir, shall we return the tent to the cellar?" a servant asked, breaking Edward's train of thought. Edward nodded and walked off toward Naomi.

"Hello, love!" Naomi called to him. "I warned them, Edward, that if they do not get to their baths immediately, you shall never read a bedtime story to them again!" she laughed.

Edward offered a brief grin.

Naomi called to the remaining servant, "You may take down the little kites from the posts, now!"

Jeanie objected immediately, "Please, no, mum. Please leave'm. They are verra bonnie."

"All right, for one more day, but I am not sure how they shall hold up in the rain," Naomi warned. "On second thought, leave them!" she instructed the servant.

Beatrice intervened, "Come along girls. There will not be enough time for Mr. McDonnally to read to you, if you do not hustle along. Make haste!"

Out of breath, Naomi smiled at her brood running ahead of her mother.

"Edward, it has been a glorious day!"

"Yes, love. Shall we take a walk?"

"Feeling neglected, you sweet man?"

Edward put his arm around her shoulders, "Never." After a short distance, Edward spoke calmly, "Naomi, I received a wire today."

"You did? Who sent it?"

Edward stopped and faced her.

"Love, Bruce and Maryanne have been released from the hospital. They will be returning with the baby to collect the girls."

Naomi was stunned. She had not expected their return to be so soon. She stood frozen and distant. She finally mouthed the word *when*.

"Tomorrow."

Naomi turned to hide her tears. She stared at the blur of multi-colored kites fluttering on the posts and mumbled, "That is very good news."

Edward embraced her and closed his eyes when she began trembling in his arms.

He said softly, "I know love, we shall miss them; the house shall be a frightfully quiet. Dear, it shan't be long before Allison has a brother or sister."

He cupped Naomi's tear-streaked face in his hands. "We need to share this good news with the girls. Can you do this?"

Naomi laid her head against Edward's chest for a few more minutes, and then looked up with a half-hearted smile. "I thank God for having had the opportunity and the experience," she said sadly.

Edward nodded. They put on their most convincing smiles, entered their home. Holding Dara, Edward informed Wilmoth, Corinne, Marvel and Jeanie that their parents were well and coming home with Martha.

Rahzvon and Sophia spent a good portion of the remaining daylight making up for lost time. They captured the grazing horses and rode Hunter and Duff back to the barn through the vacant grounds. Sophia went to the well to clean off her shoes, while Rahzvon replaced the saddles to the racks. As he lowered Duff's head to remove the bridle, Rahzvon noticed two leather rawhide strips sticking a few inches out of the barn floor. He put the horse in the stall and got down on one knee to investigate, when Sophia entered the barn. Rahzvon looked up to her glowing face.

"Rahzvon!" She ran to him and stood with her hands folded at her chest, in a grateful position. She closed her eyes for a second and then opened them. Fighting the urge to dance ecstatically around the barn she said reverently, "I am ready."

Rahzvon glanced down at the mysterious strings and then realized his position and her expectations. *Oh no, she thinks that I am going to propose.* He stared at the dirt floor, deciding that his predicament could only be an act of God. It was His will and Rahzvon dare not avoid it any longer. He looked up at her and discreetly slid his knee over the strings. He, too, closed his eyes in a moment of prayer for the perfect words, before looking up to Sophia's beaming, hopeful expression.

"Phia, I know that this is not the most desirable or romantic location...but it *is* the place where we have spent many hours together. I confess to you that I have loved you since our first meeting in the woods. You have proven your love and your loyalty to me, a hundred times over. I hereby declare, that I love you Sophia McDonnally with all my heart and soul. I respect you, and would be proud to share my life and the Sierzik name with you, as you have shared your clan with me."

He cleared his throat and extended his trembling hand to her. He brought hers to his mouth and kissed it, as tears trickled down Sophia's cheeks. "I promise that I shall provide a good, safe home for you and our children, Phia. I shall be a loving husband and attentive, respected father. Sophia McDonnally, will you please agree to be my wife?"

Sophia wiped her tears away with the back of her hand and then nodded. To the surprise of her fiancé, Sophia then let out a scream of delight, jumped, danced and spun around until Rahzvon got to his feet. She then threw herself into his arms. Caught up in the moment, yet dazed and in shock that he had actually proposed without any plan to their future, he picked her up and carried her over to the bale by the window. The barn was silent.

With unspoken concern, he took a deep breath, "Well, Phia, it is official. *Leslew zaward skichared.*"

Their first kiss as the betrothed Mr. and Mrs. Rahzvon Sierzik promised certain commitment for an uncertain future.

"I lov'd thee from the earliest dawn
When first I saw thy beauty's ray
And will, until life's eve comes on
And beauty's blossom fades away."

—*George Moses Horton*

Non-fictional facts referenced in *Without a Sword*

A Study in Scarlet written by Sir Arthur C. Doyle
The Lost World, science fiction novel written
  by Sir Arthur Conan Doyle 1912
Popularity of: perfume atomizer, hatpin, glove box
  hair combs and shell hairpins
Alice Roosevelt, President T. Roosevelt's daughter,
  America's sweetheart, outgoing, accomplished
  woman whose likeness is seen as the famous,
  admired, "Gibson Girl"— ink drawings by artist
  Charles Dana Gibson.
Graham's Magazine featuring Edgar A. Poe's,
  The Murders in the Rue Morgue
Trollhiemen Mountains '*home of the* (mythical)
  Trolls in Norway.
Buckhorn, Norwegian instrument
Adonis myth
Suffrage dates: Finland, Norway and New Zealand
Running of the Bulls in Spain
Michelangelo's statue *David*
Emma—novel by Jane Austen (1877)
New York Metropolitan Opera
The Delineator Romance Magazine passage
Hubert- inventor of flashlight
German saying repeated by Allison
  in *To Each his Own* chapter
World's Fair in St. Louis (1904) +20,000 visitors,
  featuring automatic dishwasher
Cornelius Vanderbilt's Fifth Avenue address,
  256-foot yacht *North Star*
Andrew Carnegie's residence
Jay Gould's inheritance and address
French words: *une porte, une fenêtre*
  for "one door, one window"
Italian immigrants introducing Italian ice cream

Poetry Excerpts from the Chapters

Acknowledgements

British English A to Zed.
New York: Facts on File, Inc., 2001

Chronicle of the 20th Century.
New York: Chronicle Publications, 1987

Grun, Bernard. The Timetables of History: A
Horizontal Linkage of People and Events.
New York: Simon and Schuster, 1982.

Illustrated Encyclopedia of Scotland.
Anacortes: Oyster Press, 2004.

Kidd, Dorothy. To See Ourselves. Edinburgh:
HarperCollins, 1992

Kirkby, Mandy. Pick Your Brains About Scotland.
London: Cargan Guides, 2005

Lacayo, Richard & Russell, George. Eyewitness
150 Years of Journalism.
 New York: Time Inc. Magazine Company, 1995.

Lundy, Derek. The Way of a Ship.
New York: HarperCollins Publishers, Inc., 2002

Summers, Gilbert. Exploring Rural Scotland.
Lincolnwood: Passport Books, 1996

This Fabulous Century Volume I.
New York: Time-Life Books, 1969

Webster's International Encyclopedia.
Naples: Trident Press International, 1996.

Webster's New Biographical Dictionary.
Springfield: Merriam-Webster Inc, 1988.

Webster's New Explorer Desk Encyclopedia.
Springfield, MA: Federal Street Press, 2003

I am a firm believer that education
should be an ongoing endeavor.
I stand by the unwritten law that education
should be entertaining for young and old, alike.
Thus, I incorporate
historic places, people, and events in my novels,
for your learning pleasure.

With loving thoughts,
Arianna Snow

To order copies
of the
Lochmoor Glen Series

Visit the
Golden Horse Ltd.
website:

www.ariannaghnovels.com

Watch for the
next in the series!